THE SLOPES OF LOVE

Recovering from a broken engagement, Karen Miller takes a job as resort representative at St. Wilhelm in Austria. Working at the Hotel Adler, she finds herself constantly at odds with the owner, the cold and distant Karl Braun. The guests arrive for the Christmas and New Year holidays, but behind the jollity of the festivities lurks danger — a sinister threat reaching out from England — which Karen must face alone in the cold darkness of the mountain.

Books by Diney Delancey
in the Linford Romance Library:

FOR LOVE OF OLIVER
AN OLD-FASHIONED LOVE
LOVE'S DAWNING
SILVERSTRAND
BRAVE HEART

DINEY DELANCEY

THE SLOPES OF LOVE

Complete and Unabridged

LINFORD
Leicester

First published in Great Britain in 1981 by
Robert Hale Limited
London

First Linford Edition
published 2007
by arrangement with
Robert Hale Limited
London

British Library CIP Data

Delancey, Diney
The slopes of love.—Large print ed.—
Linford romance library
1. Love stories
2. Large type books
I. Title
823.9′14 [F]

ISBN 978–1–84617–641–8

F. A. Thorpe (Publishing)
Set by Words & Graphics Ltd.
T. J. International Ltd., Padstow, Cornwall

This book is printed on acid-free paper

For Joanna.

1

'I'm sorry to speak so frankly,' said Marianne, looking across the fireplace at her sister slumped in an armchair opposite her, 'but it's about time somebody did. Look at you, Karen, you're a disgrace.' Karen Miller, who had been gazing unseeing into the heart of the log fire and only partly listening to Marianne, looked up in surprise at this.

'What?'

'You're pale, thin, becoming increasingly unattractive and wallowing in self-pity.'

Karen looked really startled now, but without allowing her to speak Marianne went on. 'It's time you began to snap out of it. You're not the first person in the world to have been jilted and I don't suppose you'll be the last.' Karen winced at Marianne's deliberate use of the word 'jilted' but even then Marianne did not weaken.

'Face it, Karen, Roger's gone and he's not coming back, but for goodness' sake don't go into a decline about it. You're not some willowy Victorian heroine who can't say boo to a goose. You're our Karen who's strong and determined, who takes a pride in herself and her abilities and is always such good company. Pull yourself together, love, and stop drooping about, it doesn't suit you. Get a job. Better still get your old job back; get out of that dreary bed-sitting-room and start facing facts. The world is still out there, you know, and it's time you went out to join it again.'

Karen stared in amazement as her sister delivered this diatribe. It was so unlike Marianne to make such a long speech and to be so scathing. Marianne, who had always accepted Karen's dictates even though she, Marianne, was the older sister. Meek Marianne, who could be persuaded or cajoled into anything Karen decided, was attempting to bully her younger sister. Karen found herself protesting weakly.

'It's all right for you, you're happily married. Ken comes home every evening to find you and Helen waiting for him in your own cosy little home . . . ' But Marianne cut in with unusual asperity. 'That has nothing to do with it. You're a mess — you look a mess and you're behaving like a spoilt child. I know you were heartbroken over Roger,' her face softened as she saw Karen flinch and she reached out for her sister's hand, 'but it won't do, love. You've got to sort yourself out sometime and the sooner the better. It's been two months now and that's too long to be miserable.'

Karen went home angry at her sister's interference, but with the words still echoing in the back of her mind. 'You've got to sort yourself out sometime and the sooner the better.'

Next morning, after another night of fitful sleep, Karen stared at her whey-faced reflection in the mirror. She had to admit there was a good deal of truth in what Marianne had said, truth and common sense. She studied her reflection more critically and was shocked by what she saw. Marianne had been ruthlessly honest. Her dark hair hung lankly down framing her pale unmade-up face. There were huge dark circles under her eyes from which all the sparkle had gone and her mouth was clenched into a tight straight line. She looked tired, drawn and unkempt.

'You're absolutely right, Marianne,' she spoke aloud. 'I am a disgrace,' and with sudden resolution, the first she had shown since Roger walked out, she got up to find her shampoo and to wash her hair.

As soon as her hair was dry and she was dressed, Karen threw back the curtains, opened the window and leaned out over the sill for some fresh air. It was a crisp November morning, the sun bright on the late autumn gardens and the wind flurrying the last of the fallen leaves in busy eddies along the street. A draft of smoke from a bonfire smouldering in the next garden coloured the air, and the smell of burning leaves made Karen sniff with pleasure. Recently every day had seemed as grey and dull as the last, though in fact London was enjoying a few days of autumnal warmth before winter finally set in, but from that moment a little colour began to creep back into Karen's life; she was able to catch a glimpse of the world outside still waiting for her and she found herself ready to consider the rest of Marianne's advice. She had to get a job. Heaven knows she needed the money and it did seem sensible, as first choice, to try to get her old job back. Because most of her work was abroad, helping run the package tours offered by Lambs Holidays International, she had resigned the month before she and Roger were to be married. She had planned to find other work on a nine-to-five basis so that she would have time to run their new home and look after her new husband. Now she had no job. If Lambs could not offer her anything there were plenty of other similar companies she could try and with her fluent German and intimate knowledge of Austria and its customs she should have little difficulty in finding something.

Buoyed up a little by this thought Karen turned to the telephone and dialled Lambs Holidays International — the tour operators who offer 'the world on a string'. She asked to speak to her old boss, Donald Keary, and arranged to meet him for a drink after work that evening.

When Karen arrived at the pub she thought she was first and was pleased; it would give her a minute to collect her thoughts. To help bolster her morale and because she was determined to make a good impression, she had dressed herself in one of the suits she had bought for her trousseau. It had been very expensive and Karen felt her spirits lift as she put it on, it made her feel elegant, well-dressed, its soft mulberry colour suited her and had the added advantage of bringing a little extra warmth to her otherwise pale cheeks. Smart black patent shoes and handbag completed her outfit and she looked charming. With her newly-washed hair softly curling round her ears, and her face carefully made-up, she felt better than she had since . . . She felt the familiar stab of pain and pulled herself up short, she would not think about that. What she needed now was to seem calm and efficient, a trained and experienced woman hoping to regain a job at which she had been excellent.

She paused in the doorway and several people glanced appreciatively in her direction, then Mr Keary was at her side, piloting her to a table in a corner where they could talk in peace.

'What would you like to drink?' he asked as with old-fashioned courtesy he settled her into her chair.

'Gin and tonic please,' she replied and was glad to have the few moments his journey to the bar took to calm her nerves and rehearse once more what she was going to say. Mr Keary returned with the drinks and sat down smiling. Karen found it strangely reassuring to see his familiar face with friendly brown eyes staring at her a little quizzically from under bushy grey brows and it steadied her.

'Well, Karen, this is a pleasant surprise. What can I do for you?'

Karen took a sip of her drink and then set it down carefully on the table. She returned Mr Keary's gaze for a moment before she said, 'You heard, I expect, about Roger and me. I mean, not getting married after all?'

Mr Keary nodded sympathetically. 'Yes, we were all so sorry.'

'Well,' went on Karen, 'I need a job. I thought I'd ask you first.' It came out more abruptly than she had intended, but Mr Keary did not seem unduly surprised. He merely nodded again and said, 'I see, I thought that might be it. It could be a problem.' He thought for a moment, wrinkling his nose in a look of consideration. Karen felt the chill of disappointment creeping over her as she waited for his answer.

'Of course your old job in Kitzbühel has been filled. We gave it to Sarah Morgan. Remember Sarah? Used to be on the Seefeld team. Well she'd come on well and we needed someone who could cope with a large resort. Peter and George are still there too of course, but I think Sarah will do very well.'

'I remember her,' said Karen. 'A small blonde girl.'

'That's the one. Her German's not quite as idiomatic as yours, but it's adequate. Of course your mother was Austrian, wasn't she?'

Karen nodded.

'Always helps,' said Mr Keary and lapsed into silence. Karen waited a moment and then said, brightly, 'Don't worry, Mr Keary, it was just a thought. I should have realised you'd be organised for this season.'

'Hold on a minute,' said Mr Keary with a smile, 'I didn't say there was no job. I was just explaining that your old one had gone. I agree we are practically organised for our coming winter season, but when you phoned I guessed what it was about and I had a quick chat with one or two people, and there is one possibility you might like to consider.' He paused to sip his drink. 'We've added a new resort to our lists this year; St Wilhelm in the Austrian Tyrol. Unfortunately, the man assigned there managed to break his leg playing rugby last week. It's all most inconvenient because we shall have to make a chain of alterations to cover for him, unless . . . ' he paused, 'unless you'd like to consider stepping into the breach. It could suit all of us. You'd have a job and we'd have an experienced representative in a resort we want nursed along. Are you interested?'

As he was speaking Karen felt her disappointment fade and a bubble of excitement grow within her. She drew a deep breath and said, 'Yes, very.'

'Before you get too excited about it,' went on Mr Keary, 'I must point out that it's only a one-rep village. You'll be working alone so it will be hard graft much of the time and could be lonely.'

'I think I'd like that,' said Karen.

'Maybe for a while,' agreed Mr Keary, 'but you could get very tired of it and I wouldn't be able to move you at least until this time next year. It's not the sort of job you've been doing for us, but you've plenty of general experience and if you want it the job's yours. I know you well enough to know you can cope with the practical side. It will need tact and patience, building up the social side of the operation, because I don't think Herr Braun will be an easy man to work with. Often he's charming, so I'm told, but also he's sometimes rather abrupt and gives the impression he doesn't suffer fools gladly.' Mr Keary smiled encouragingly at Karen's anxious face. 'But when all's said and done, you're not a fool.'

'Thank you,' said Karen, then she added resolutely, 'I'd like to go.'

'You don't have to make a decision on the spot,' said Mr Keary. 'Take this evening to think it over and let me know by the end of tomorrow. I'm sorry I can't give you longer, but I shall have to start the switching of schedules if you don't want to go.'

'You're very kind,' said Karen, 'but I've made up my mind already. If you're really offering me the job I'd like to take it. I need to get away from London to somewhere I'm not known. I need to work hard so that I don't have time to brood, and as you know I love Austria, it's my second home. Tell me about the place.'

Mr Keary relaxed back into his chair, glad the decision had been made.

'Well, it's a small village high up so that the skiing is excellent even until quite late in the season. New lifts have recently opened up miles of hillside, a huge skiing area which is used by two other village resorts as well. The place is going to grow as it becomes more geared to tourism and we're glad to be in from the first. The hotel we are going to use is called Hotel Adler. It is the only one of any size and its owner has gradually built it up into an excellent place to stay, of its type. Family hotel sort of thing.'

'Who is it run by?' asked Karen.

'Herr Braun. Karl Braun. A nice enough chap, as I said before, in a dour sort of way. Runs the place with his mother-in-law. Seems efficient.'

'His mother-in-law?' repeated Karen in surprise. 'Sounds an unlikely combination!'

Mr Keary smiled faintly. 'It does, but there's a good reason. Herr Braun's wife was killed in a car smash about eighteen months ago.'

'Oh, I see,' said Karen and gave a moment to wondering what sort of man could run a hotel with his mother-in-law. Perhaps it was she who ran both hotel and Herr Braun. Then she realised Mr Keary was speaking again and turned her attention back to him.

'You'll have a room at the hotel and there is a kiosk in the entrance hall for your office.'

'You mean I actually live in the hotel? That's unusual.'

'Well, they were prepared to allow us the room and it seemed sensible to have you on the spot, particularly as you're on your own and all your guests will be at the one hotel. Herr Braun was keen our representative should be in the hotel to ensure the smooth running of the holidays. Herr Braun really wanted . . . Well, that doesn't matter. Keep everything going easily and efficiently and you'll stay on the right side of Herr Braun. He's only contracted for this one season, and we don't want to lose the hotel to another company next year.'

'I'll do my best,' said Karen, still a little dazed by the whole proposition.

Mr Keary patted her hand. 'I'm sure you will, my dear. That's settled then.

Come into the office tomorrow and we'll sort out the formalities. You'll have to go pretty soon as it's a new resort to sort out the après-ski possibilities, etc. You'll have a fairly free hand there, to establish a routine and organise the various entertainments for the season. There's plenty more bumph on the place in the office, so you can do some more detailed homework before you leave.' He got to his feet and downed what was left of his drink. 'I must dash,' he said. 'Sorry I can't stay longer, but I promised my wife I wouldn't be too late. See you in the morning!' and he disappeared out into the November evening.

Karen sat nursing her drink, hardly touched, shaken by the speed of it all yet excited by the job in prospect. She had been a tour rep with Lambs for six years and had graduated through the smaller resorts to the large resort of Kitzbühel where there were four permanent reps. But she had never been her own boss before; never broken new ground without a more experienced representative on hand to guide her. St Wilhelm. It would be a chance to immerse herself in work, and the responsibility for the whole village, though heavy, was welcome. She would answer the challenge of breaking new ground, building up contacts with the local people to give her guests a chance to become, for a week or so, part of an Austrian village. She had been given a free hand to establish the hotel and the resort as a Lambs recommended holiday and her organising spirit rose in anticipation. 'I can make a success of this job,' she thought enthusiastically. 'I'll make it work, with or in spite of Herr Karl Braun and his mother-in-law.'

And with the bubble of excitement continuing to grow within her, Karen too downed her drink and went out into the chill of the November evening to telephone Marianne and tell her she had begun the long climb back.

2

The next few days were hectic as Karen prepared to leave for St Wilhelm. Marianne had been thrilled about the job and helped Karen get herself ready. Her parting words were those of love and encouragement. 'Don't forget to keep in touch regularly, you know we'll be longing to hear how the job goes, what the village is like and everything.' She gave her sister a final hug. 'I'm sure you're doing the right thing, Karen; I've a feeling this job at St Wilhelm will give you the chance you need and I'm green with envy to think you'll be skiing every day. Take care, love.'

'I will,' said Karen, 'and I'll write soon.'

So everything was arranged, the goodbyes said, and Karen was on her way at last. She flew to Munich, took a train to Innsbruck and then had to decide whether to struggle on by bus or blow the expense and take a taxi. She decided on the taxi and dropped into the back seat, relieved to be on the last leg of her journey. It was a cold December afternoon roofed by a leaden sky, threatening snow; and though she knew there were mountains all round they were shrouded in a light shifting mist and she had only fleeting glimpses of their rocky walls. The road soon left the valley floor and began its tortuous climb up the mountainside. They passed through several villages, many no more than a knot of houses clinging to the hillside and dominated by a thin-spired church, and then wound their way through pine-trees still and dark, almost menacing the road. Several times the road was so narrow that when they met oncoming traffic, one or other vehicle had to reverse. Karen noticed it was rarely the taxi; her driver gave way only to buses and lorries, the rest of the time he forged ahead, his horn blaring a two-tone tune at each hairpin bend, but seldom slowing to negotiate the actual turn.

At last, with the valley lost in mist below them, the driver called cheerfully, 'Here we are, fräulein. This is St Wilhelm and here's the hotel.' And he swung into a tiny village square. Houses with wide eaves, long balconies and painted shutters formed three sides of the square and on the fourth was Karen's destination, the Hotel Adler. The taxi pulled into the hotel forecourt and the driver jumped out to unload Karen's luggage. Karen climbed out stiffly, glad to arrive before the gathering dusk finally turned to darkness. The hotel looked warm and welcoming, with lights gleaming from the front door and several windows. It too had the wide sweeping roof of the other houses and the painted shutters folded back against the white walls. Under the windows were wide sills for summer window-boxes, and a huge mural of a soaring eagle was painted to one side of the front door, over which were the words, Hotel Adler. Karen paid off the taxi and when he had driven off into the twilight, his horn blaring at the first corner, she stood for a moment and surveyed the place that was to be her home for the next months. It looked warm and comfortable and the smell of woodsmoke on the evening air promised open fires indoors. Lights were twinkling in many houses now and several people crossed the square hurrying home to their firesides. Karen picked up her cases and, leaving her skis in a rack by the front door, went inside. An immediate glow of warmth enveloped her and as the door swung closed behind her, a grey-haired woman came from a room off the entrance hall with an enquiring smile.

'Good-evening, can I help you?'

'Yes, my name's Karen Miller, I'm the Lambs International representative.'

'Ah, Miss Miller, we've been expecting you. How do you do? I'm Frau Leiter the manageress. My son-in-law and I run the hotel together.'

They shook hands and Karen said, 'How do you do?'

'We're so pleased to welcome you here,' went on Frau Leiter. 'What a pity to arrive on such a horrible evening, but the forecast is better for tomorrow and soon we should get some snow. Now I'll show you upstairs.'

She led the way across the panelled hall and up a staircase with beautifully carved wooden banisters. The landing too was pine-panelled and each bedroom door let into the panelling matched exactly. At the end of the landing Frau Leiter opened one of these doors and stood aside to let Karen into the room.

'What a pretty room!' Karen exclaimed, putting her cases down and looking round.

'It's very simple and rather small,' apologised Frau Leiter, 'but at least it's your own, a refuge for you when you need one.' She smiled. 'I'll leave you to unpack, come down when you are ready and have something to eat, I'm sure you're hungry. The bathroom's second on the left along the landing.'

'Thank you,' said Karen. 'I'll be down soon.'

Frau Leiter closed the door and Karen sat down on her bed and took stock of her 'refuge'. It was simple, but warm, cosy and welcoming. The bed along one wall, was covered with a cheerful red-checked continental quilt. Beside it stood a small chest of drawers with a lamp on top. There was a table and chair by the window, a basin with a mirror over it in one corner and a built-in cupboard in another. That was all, but she needed no more. The curtains matched the quilt cover and Karen crossed to draw them against the darkness which was now complete outside. As she did so, she heard raised voices and looked down into the courtyard below. Her room overlooked the square and the hotel forecourt and it was there that she saw two men arguing. Standing in the courtyard, clearly lit by a shaft of light from an open door, a tall man was in angry conversation with the driver of a lorry parked across the hotel entrance. The argument was fierce and the raised voices carried up to Karen's window, though the double glazing muffled exactly what was said. Suddenly the tall man turned on his heel and the light from the doorway fell bright on his face. Karen pressed her nose against the window to get a better view of him. He was good-looking, almost handsome, with clean-cut regular features and rather a square jaw, but his eyes were hard and his mouth set in an angry line. His dark hair was thick and straight and he tossed it in irritation as he strode back towards the hotel. 'That must be Karl Braun,' thought Karen, 'and he's the one I've got to work with. I hope he doesn't lose his temper like that too often.' As she watched him he seemed to sense her gaze and glanced up at her window. She drew back at once and pulled the curtains, but she was sure he had seen her and for some reason it made her feel at a disadvantage; as if she had been caught spying.

'That's stupid,' she told herself, 'I haven't even met the man. Well, he's not going to boss me about,' she thought determinedly. 'I'm my own boss, and if necessary I'll let him know it.'

After she had washed and changed into a comfortable sweater-dress of dark green, Karen decided the time had come to go downstairs and find something to eat as Frau Leiter had suggested and of course, she added lightly, to meet Herr Karl Braun. She went along the landing and started downstairs, but as she came to the turn in the staircase she heard voices in the hall below. Hearing her own name mentioned Karen paused on the half-landing, out of sight, and listened.

'She seems very pleasant, quiet and sensible.' Frau Leiter was saying.

'But can she do the job? It's no good if she's not well organised.' The man's voice was irritable. 'I won't have standards drop. We need someone with a positive and imaginative approach.'

'How do I know if she's well organised? For goodness' sake, Karl, she's only been here half an hour! Wait and judge for yourself.'

'I will,' said the man ominously, 'and if it doesn't work out she'll have to go. I wanted a man here. I told Keary so. It's too much for a mere girl. I saw her at the window. A mere girl.'

Karen felt an angry flush rising to her cheeks and had to fight to stop herself from marching down the stairs to confront that pompous man and tell him what she thought of male chauvinists like him. However, common sense prevailed and with the whisper of Mr Keary's warning about tact and patience echoing in her head she counted to ten and then continued downstairs to find Frau Leiter and to meet Herr Braun; but in the latter she was disappointed. Frau Leiter was alone in the hall. She smiled as Karen appeared and said, 'There you are, my dear, come along

I'll show you round.'

Frau Leiter took Karen through the hotel's public rooms.

'The guests have many facilities here,' she said. 'This bar is small and quite cosy, just right for a quiet drink before dinner or a glühwein after skiing.'

It was a most attractive bar and Karen loved it at once. It was panelled and many of the wooden panels had alpine scenes painted on them. There was a large wood-burning stove in one corner and the tables and chairs were set with this as the focal point rather than the bar itself. She could imagine happy groups of people, flushed and excited from a day's skiing, flopped into the chairs sipping the hot mulled wine, glühwein, so comforting and restoring after a day of hard exercise, and laughingly swapping stories of how they had fared on the slopes.

Frau Leiter led her back into the hall and pointed to a staircase leading down to the hotel's basement.

'That's the 'keller-bar' downstairs where there's music and any parties are held. Over here is the lounge.' She led the way into a large room furnished with low coffee-tables, comfortable chairs and sofas. Here there was an open fireplace with the embers of a log fire smouldering gently in its hearth.

'What a lovely room!' exclaimed Karen.

'I'm glad you approve.' Karl Braun's voice made her spin round in surprise. He was standing in the doorway behind them, unashamedly looking Karen over as if noting her general appearance. It seemed to meet with his approval for he gave a slight nod before moving forward to introduce himself. Seeing him again, this time face to face, Karen reassessed her first impression of him. He was good-looking, as she had originally thought, but his eyes held no warmth and consequently his face was not attractive. He smiled politely as he held out his hand, but his smile held no warmth either.

'Karl Braun. This is my hotel. I see you are already friends with my mother-in-law. I hope you'll be happy here. If we work together I am sure all will be well.'

'You didn't think that five minutes ago!' Karen longed to retort, but, mindful of her promise to Donald Keary, she merely smiled back at him and agreed.

'We'll get down to business tomorrow,' he said turning. 'Just relax this evening and recover from your journey.' His look dismissed her and he spoke to Frau Leiter.

'Have you seen Marta, Mother?'

'No, Karl, I don't think she's back yet.'

'Well, it's time she was. She should come straight home.'

'Maybe the bus was late,' said Frau Leiter soothingly. 'It's Friday, she can do her homework at the weekend. You mustn't worry about her so much. She is sixteen, you know.'

'Well, tell her I want her when she

comes in,' said Karl. 'I'll be in the office,' and he left them.

Frau Leiter showed Karen the dining-room and pointed out a small table in a corner by the door.

'That's yours, my dear. Karl feels you should take your meals with the guests so you're on hand should there be any problem.'

'He obviously thinks I'm a slave to my guests,' thought Karen angrily. 'I can't even snatch a meal in peace.'

'However,' continued Frau Leiter, 'as you have no clients yet, we'd be pleased if you'd join the family this evening. Marta, my granddaughter, will be home from school at any moment and we shall eat at about seven. Karl eats later because he's supervising the dining-room.'

Karen thanked her and accepted the offer of family supper, but was secretly pleased Karl would not be there. Until she had a chance to show him she was as efficient and competent as any male representative would have been, she felt she would be happier keeping well clear of him.

Supper was a cheerful meal and Karen took to Karl's daughter, Marta, immediately. She was shy but friendly and complimented Karen on her German.

'Well, I have an advantage. My mother was Austrian and my sister, Marianne, and I were brought up bilingual.'

'That is an advantage,' agreed Frau Leiter. 'Marta's learning English at school. Perhaps you'll let her practise on you occasionally.'

Marta blushed with embarrassment. 'Oma, please! Fräulein Miller won't have time for English lessons.'

'Of course we'll have time, all we need to do is chat in English and you'll find you improve by leaps and bounds; and please call me Karen, it's so much nicer when we are going to be seeing so much of each other.'

'There you are,' said Frau Leiter. 'Karen doesn't mind, and it would please your father so much if your English improved.'

'That's settled then,' agreed Karen. 'You talk English when you like and I'll help you when you go wrong. In return you can help me. I need to know all about St Wilhelm and what goes on here and you can tell me. And when the snow comes you can guide me round the mountain and show me all the runs. That would be marvellous.'

'Oh yes, I'd love to,' exclaimed Marta. 'Are you a good skier?' Then she blushed at the question. 'I'm sorry I didn't mean . . . '

Karen laughed. 'Don't worry, I've skied most of my life, we used to come over and spend Christmas with my grandparents; never fear, I'll keep up.'

Marta smiled, then said, a little tentatively, 'We could walk tomorrow if you like. Take the chairlift up and walk the trail down again.'

'That would be great,' said Karen. 'I have to do some work with your father in the morning, but I don't expect to be with him for long the first time, and it would be marvellous to get to know the village and the mountains.'

Marta seemed quite excited at the prospect and Frau Leiter said, 'You'd better get your homework done tonight if you're going out tomorrow.'

Karen did not stay up long after supper. She suddenly felt exhausted and longed to collapse into bed, so she said goodnight to Marta who was struggling with her homework and to Frau Leiter and went upstairs. It was only as she reached the landing that she remembered her skis. She had left them in the rack outside the front door. Not wanting to leave them there all night she went downstairs again to move them. Frau Leiter had told her where the ski-locker-room was, down a flight of outside steps at the back of the hotel, so she slipped out of the front door to collect the skis and put them away. The coldness of the night air made her gasp as she stepped outside. She had not bothered to fetch her coat and the cold cut through to her skin. Quickly, she picked up her skis and, shouldering them, followed the path round the hotel and down the dark steps to the ski-room. There was no light and she had to feel her way down the stone stairs. At the bottom she put out her hand to open the door she knew must be there and touched, not a door as she had expected, but a person. Half-screaming, she leapt back and her skis clattered to the ground.

'Steady!' said Karl Braun's voice. 'Is that you, Fräulein Miller?'

'Yes. What on earth are you doing lurking in the dark?' Karen's shock made her angry and she snapped at him irritably.

'I'm not lurking.' His voice sounded faintly amused. 'I'm locking up. I do every night, you know. Is that all right?' He spoke humouringly as if to a child and his tone made her even angrier. She took a deep breath and then said in a tightly controlled voice, 'I brought my skis down, to put them away.'

'Very sensible,' he said as he reached in and turned on the ski-room light. It shone on her skis and he picked them up for her.

'I'll put them inside. They're nice skis, you shouldn't go throwing them around, you know.' His voice was teasing but Karen was too angry at her own carelessness to respond to his tone. She snapped back, 'I didn't throw them down on purpose. It was your fault.'

'Of course,' he soothed. 'Have you done a lot of skiing?' Karen had not minded when Marta had asked her the same question, but somehow she resented it from Karl Braun. She answered tersely, 'Yes, all my life.'

'That's good,' he said, 'you'll find some excellent runs here, some of them really testing. Your skis'll be safe in here,' he added and locked the ski-room door.

'Thank you,' said Karen and turned to grope her way back up the dark stairs. Karl took her arm and piloted her back into the welcoming warmth of the hotel.

'You shouldn't come outside without a coat,' he said, 'you're shivering.'

Karen had forgotten the cold in her fright and anger, now she discovered he was right and she was freezing. Once inside he dropped her arm and made a mock bow.

'Goodnight, Fräulein Miller. Sleep well, I'll see you in the morning.'

'Goodnight, Herr Braun,' and Karen, trying to be composed and dignified, walked slowly upstairs. When she reached the sanctuary of her room she flung herself on her bed shaking with anger, at him and more so at herself. Again she remembered the words of Donald Keary, 'Herr Braun doesn't give the impression that he suffers fools gladly.' Well, she wasn't a fool, but she had done nothing to demonstrate that fact to Herr Braun so far, indeed rather the opposite. And Donald Keary might have warned her Karl Braun had asked for a man. Never mind, tomorrow when they really got down to business, she would be able to show him that she was more than up to her job and that she had the positive and imaginative approach he wanted; but before she could think of any suggestions, particularly positive or imaginative ones, Karen fell into a sleep of exhaustion and remained sleeping dreamlessly until morning.

3

Karen awoke to a glorious morning. The sun streamed in through a crack in her curtains and when she threw them open the view which greeted her quite took her breath away. Gone were the wreaths of mist which had shrouded the mountains the evening before. Now they towered around the village, their harsh grey crags jutting sharply against a slate-blue sky. The square immediately below was bathed in sunlight, showing up the painting on the white walls of some of the houses and the beautiful carving on some of the eaves. The square sloped away from her and beyond, between the houses, Karen could see the distant valley floor far below. She struggled with the double windows and then flung them wide to admit a draught of exhilarating mountain air. It was cold and clear and it seemed to Karen as she drew a deep and lingering breath that it cleared her head and things which had been worrying her no longer loomed large, but slipped back into proportion. She could cope.

She dressed quickly and hurried downstairs for breakfast. Black coffee and beautifully fresh bread rolls completed the tonic and she felt ready to face anything, including Karl Braun.

He was waiting for her in the hall and after a brief 'good-morning' led her through to his office. He set a chair for her and settled himself behind his desk.

'Now, Karen, I may call you Karen, mayn't I? I gather Marta and my mother-in-law already do.'

'Yes, please do.'

'Well, if you could give me an outline of the programmes you'd like to offer your guests, we'll see what we can arrange.' Karen had made some notes before leaving England and she started from these.

'Well, we want our guests to be as

free as possible, able to come and go as they choose, join in or not with arranged skiing and entertainments.'

'I agree with that in principle,' said Karl, 'perhaps you could go into more detail.'

Karen could and did and, an hour and a half later, she and Karl had drawn up an outline programme for the season and the extra festivities for Christmas and the New Year; including traditional carol-singing in the square on Christmas Eve and a fancy-dress party on New Year's Eve.

They had worked well together and Karen was aware of an easing of the strange tension between them. Karl looked across at her as she put away her notebook.

'That all sounds very promising,' he said. 'If you run into any problems don't hesitate to ask. We're here to do the best we can for the guests and, working together, we could make a good job of it.' His eyes held hers for a moment as he smiled and suddenly he was completely altered; his face lost its harsh heaviness and the anxious lines were replaced by the crinkles of laughter. Karen was shaken by the transformation but it was as fleeting as it was surprising, and his face immediately reverted to its normal serious self.

For some stupid reason Karen felt her own face colouring and said hastily, 'I have to see the ski-school director now. Can you tell me where he works from?'

'Of course, he runs a bar across the square and down the alley on the left. Johann Schultz.'

'Thank you, I have his name,' said Karen stiffly. She did not want Karl to think she had come unprepared.

Karl rose to his feet and said equally stiffly, 'Then I won't keep you,' and feeling like a dismissed schoolgirl Karen found herself back in the hall, the easiness gone and tension returned. She was about to go out to find Johann's bar, when Marta bounced down the stairs.

‘Are you going out, Karen, to explore the village? Can I come too?’

‘Of course,’ said Karen. ‘I’m just off to find Herr Johann Schultz to discuss the ski-school.’

‘Oh, Johann, I’ll show you where he lives. Come on.’

They stepped out into the sparkling morning. It was very cold and the air was piercingly sharp, but so invigorating that the shadow in which Karen had been left after Karl’s abrupt departure lifted and she stood in the square for a moment, overcome by the magnificence of the mountains and the strange exhilaration their towering presence gave her.

Marta pointed out the chairlift and the new cable-car. ‘The chair has been here for years,’ she explained. ‘It is in two sections, you can just see the middle station if you look up there.’

Karen looked and saw the line of pylons running up the hillside, between the trees and up again to a small group of buildings.

'There's a restaurant there too,' went on Marta, 'with a fantastic view. It's only popular at lunchtime with skiers who don't want to come down to the village to eat.'

Karen made a mental note of this, thinking she might organise a voucher system for her own guests who were on full board at the hotel.

'The cable-car goes across to the other side,' said Marta. 'It links in with the drag-lift system in a sort of bowl area above Feldkirch and Rheindorf, the next two villages. You can ski right back down to each of the villages from the top of the cable car, or you can go by mini-bus to one of the others, ride up their lift system and ski back down here. That's quite a good day out too.'

Karen made a mental note of that as well.

They continued round the square and Marta turned into a little alley that was so narrow it was almost roofed by the eaves of the houses on either side. A sign hung on one wall, announcing

'Johann's', and she pushed open the door below it and led Karen into a bar. It was deserted.

'Johann,' called Marta. 'Johann, are you there?' A door at the back opened and a young man of about twenty-five appeared. He was tall and his fair hair was long and flopped across his forehead. His eyes were of the most brilliant blue Karen had ever seen, sparkling even in the dim light of the empty bar-room. His face cracked into an easy smile of welcome. 'Marta! Come in. Who's this you've brought with you?'

Marta performed the introductions and Johann led them through the bar into a cosy sitting-room at the back. Seated in a chair was a younger man who leapt to his feet when he saw Karen and Marta.

'This is my young cousin, Hans-Peter,' said Johann. 'He's come from Vienna to work as a ski-instructor over the Christmas period, down from university for a month. He's studying modern languages. His English is excellent.'

Hans-Peter smiled and Karen saw at once that he must be the devastation of his year at the university, for although his smile was charming he also had dark moody eyes, a heartbreaker without doubt. One glance at Marta confirmed her thoughts but she had no time for further wondering as Johann claimed her attention again.

'Now then, Fräulein Miller . . . '

'Karen, please.'

'Karen, thank you. Let me tell you about the ski-school. It only operates in the winter of course.' He smiled and added, 'But the bar is popular all the year, I'm glad to say.' Karen explained her business and Johann, who had already been approached by Lambs when they had visited St Wilhelm originally, was ready with plans to accommodate her guests.

'It's all very easy. My father started the ski-school years ago for St Wilhelm only, but it gradually expanded and now we are quite a big ski-school because we serve the smaller villages round the hill, Feldkirch and Rheindorf, as well.'

'Your father no longer takes an active part?' asked Karen, who had been surprised to find the ski-school director so young.

'My father died last year,' explained Johann.

'Oh, I'm sorry, I didn't realise,' said Karen, wishing now that she had allowed Karl to tell her about Johann after all.

'Of course you didn't,' smiled Johann, 'don't worry. And now I run both the ski-school and the bar myself.'

It did not take long to conclude the details and then Johann produced coffee. After all her negotiating that morning, Karen felt she needed it and allowed herself to be tempted by one of the beautiful apple pastries he offered as well.

'We're going up the chair this afternoon,' said Marta. 'Why don't you both come too, Johann? Karen wants to learn the mountains before the snow comes.'

'She'll have to be quick then,' said Johann. 'There was a sprinkling on the top this morning. It'll be here soon.'

'Well, will you come this afternoon?'

'Sounds a good idea, eh, Hans-Peter?' said Johann with his easy smile. 'We'll see you at the chair at about two.'

The chairlift station stood just above the village, about three minutes' walk from the hotel. When Karen and Marta reached it, they found Johann and Hans-Peter waiting for them.

'Wait for us at the middle station,' Johann said, as Karen and Marta stepped into the slowly moving chairs. Karen was glad it was a single chairlift. Marta was a sweet girl, but Karen wanted to be alone to enjoy the solitude of the mountainside, the silence only punctuated by the clunk of the cable at each pylon. The peace she had felt so often before when swinging slowly up the hillside on a chairlift swept over her again. Everyday worries seemed unimportant, as unimportant as she herself, a swinging dot amid the grandeur of the mountains. The chair passed through the serried ranks of silent firs, the light scarcely penetrating their thick, motionless branches. In one place, there was a wide track through the trees and Marta, calling from the chair behind, said, 'That's one of the runs down to the village. It's quite steep and narrow in places but it's marvellous coming through the trees.'

Karen waved and turned back to find the ground rising so steeply in front of her that she was only about six feet off the ground. 'One could almost get off there,' she thought. The chair swung on upwards, beyond the trees and over open pasture-land until it reached the middle station. There she waited for the others. She was glad when they arrived. The sky had clouded over and with no sun to give its fleeting warmth Karen found herself shivering, although she was well wrapped up in trousers, anorak and thick fur boots. She took a woolly ski-hat from her pocket and pulled it on, down over her ears.

'We can't go any higher today,' announced Johann, 'at least not if we're going to walk down. The snow'll be here tonight and we must be down well before dark. If you want to go higher we'll have to take the chair both ways.'

'No, let's walk,' said Karen. 'I'm very unfit and it'll do me good.' She looked down the mountain. She could see the bottom station, where they had got on the lift, and it seemed a long way down. Johann handed her some binoculars. 'I brought these,' he said. 'I thought you might like to use them.'

'Thank you,' breathed Karen. 'It is a fantastic view.' She scanned the valley below her and found she could easily pick out The Adler and the square and at the bottom station she could even see men moving about on the platform where the chairs were mounted.

'Come on,' said Johann, 'we must start down.' Hans-Peter, who had been stamping his feet, set off in the lead quickly followed by Marta, leaving Johann and Karen to follow. As soon as they were moving, Karen felt warmer and really began to enjoy herself. The track led across the hillside and then dipped down steeply into the trees. Several times it crossed the path of the chairlift and the ever-moving cable of chairs passed silently overhead. Occasionally there was a break in the trees to display the most magnificent panorama of mountains and the patchwork valley floor. Johann was entertaining company, full of stories about skiing and the village and its unsuspecting villagers. Karen found herself opening up to his easy friendship and, before she realised what she was saying, telling him about the excitement of her new job and how she longed to do really well and then, of all things, about Roger, and realised with a sudden jolt that it was the first time Roger had entered her thoughts since she had arrived in Austria. Johann was encouraging and sympathetic.

'You mustn't let old Karl Braun get you down,' he said, after she had told him how keen she was to succeed in her job. 'Oh, I know you haven't said he's difficult,' he added, as she began to protest, 'you wouldn't, but he's not been the same man since Anna was killed. It seems to have killed something in him too. And he's always worried about Marta, afraid he's not bringing her up properly on his own. Frau Leiter says . . . ' but Karen did not learn what Frau Leiter said because he broke off as Marta came back up the path towards them.

'You two are dawdling,' she complained, 'we're miles ahead of you. Come on, Karen, come and see the view as we come right out of the trees. It looks most peculiar.'

Karen and Johann hurried to catch them up and to see the strange view; the valley floor was now lost as a layer of mist or cloud had spread over it; and there as if floating on a cloud was St Wilhelm.

'Doesn't it look eerie?' said Marta. 'Like a ghost village.'

'That mist'll be up here soon,' said Johann. 'Let's get a move on. You'll be skiing this time next week, Karen.'

As they reached St Wilhelm, Marta and Hans-Peter went on ahead again, leaving Karen and Johann to find their way through the village in the gathering dusk. Johann took Karen's arm to pilot her through the unfamiliar little alleys and outside his bar he suddenly turned her towards him, pulling her against him and kissed her gently, first on the forehead and then on the lips.

'Remember,' he said, as he raised his head and looked down into her startled eyes. 'Remember, you're welcome at the bar any time you need to escape, and if you need help don't be afraid to ask. We want you to feel at home here.' He made to kiss her again, but Karen pulled away, saying quickly, 'Thank you, Johann, I'll remember. I'll certainly come to see you. And thank you for this afternoon.'

She half waved and stumbled off across the square, too astonished at what had happened to notice the first snowflakes drifting silently through the evening air. Marta was waiting outside the hotel and they hurried inside, glad to be out of the cold.

Frau Leiter was very relieved to see them and hustled them into the family living room to nurse a cup of hot chocolate and toast their toes by the fire.

'Your father was worried about you, Marta,' she scolded gently. 'You'd better go and tell him you're back safely.'

Marta pulled a face. 'He fusses too much,' she said grumpily.

'Only because he's fond of you, darling,' said her grandmother. 'Go on, be a good girl and tell him.'

Marta went off to do so and Frau Leiter said to Karen, 'He does worry too much, sometimes about the wrong things and not enough about the right things. I don't mean to be disloyal, but

I worry about him too. He never used to flare up the way he does. I feel I must warn you, he won't be an easy man to work with.'

Karen thanked her. 'I understand, I know about his wife. We'll manage all right.'

4

Johann's prediction about Karen's skiing by the next weekend proved correct. Indeed, by the next morning, there were several inches of snow and the fall continued for a further twenty-four hours and then intermittently throughout the week.

The snow transformed the village from an attractive study in browns and greys and green to an icing-sugar creation of gleaming icicles and frosted windows, with all unevenness smoothed away under the shining blanket of white. The character of the village changed overnight, the winter village immediately replacing the summer one. Tractors were out gritting the roads and a plough was clearing the drifts to make sure St Wilhelm was not cut off from the valley. Attention was given to the snow on the ski-runs and soon work was progressing, packing it ready for the arrival of the tourists. The locals were out immediately and the chairlift and cable-cars ran all day.

Karen completed all the arrangements for the hire of equipment for her guests, which had been arranged in outline by the company. She was determined to get to know the people she had to deal with personally, so that any problems could be dealt with quickly and easily. Johann was a great help, introducing her casually to the villagers who frequented his bar and incidentally booking a regular evening out for her guests to 'meet the locals' there. She had her kiosk set up in the hotel hall and posted as much local information as she had been able to collect. Karl nodded his approval and Karen knocked up another point to her efficiency and was pleased.

Karen saw little of Marta that week, though the girl was at school in the daytime and trailing admiringly after Hans-Peter in the evenings. When Karl commented on this to Frau Leiter, his mother-in-law said gently, 'She's nearly seventeen, Karl.'

'Well, her schoolwork must not suffer,' said Karl testily, but he merely told Marta she had to be in by ten thirty, and she escaped the lecture he might have given.

Karen's first guests arrived the next Saturday, but she was able to try several of the ski-runs before she had to collect a coach and go to the airport to meet them.

She felt the usual thrill of exhilaration as she slid off the chairlift at the middle station and heard the whisper of the snow under her skis. She swept off down the hill, the air whistling past her face as she turned and followed the trail they had walked through the woods.

She did not hear him coming, but suddenly she found another skier at her side. Glancing across, she saw it was Karl. He grinned and waved her to follow him as he accelerated past her and, leaving the marked trail, cut down through the trees. Determined not to be outdone, Karen also left the trail and shot through the trees behind him, following his tracks in the snow as closely as she could. It was not easy and, though she would hardly admit it even to herself, Karen was glad when Karl schussed to a stop to wait for her.

He grinned at her boyishly, as she hissed to a standstill beside him. 'You're very good,' he cried, 'quite worthy of those beautiful skis.'

Karen was a little out of breath, which was probably a good thing as she was not able to make the cutting remark which had risen to her lips, before Karl went on. 'I like to see a woman ski well. You have a neat smooth style. My wife, Anna, was a first-class skier too.'

Relief that she had not blurted out her snub flooded through Karen as she realised he was paying her an honest compliment. Her face, already flushed from the exhilaration of the run, took an even deeper tone. Karl smiled his startling smile, the one Karen had only seen once before, and thought of privately as his 'real smile'. She felt her own smile return his.

'Come on,' he said. 'I'll show you a fabulous run back from here. It ends the other side of the village, I'm afraid, so we'll have to walk home, but it's worth it if you're game.'

'I'm right behind you,' sang out Karen and they turned down the mountain once more.

Karen went to collect her guests with a curiously light heart. Everything seemed to be going like clockwork. The skiing was fantastic, the arrangements for the guests seemed in order, various entertainments had been organised, but none of these quite accounted for the sudden overwhelming feeling of well-being Karen felt on her way to the airport.

It was short-lived.

The flight from London was two hours late; and when it did arrive there was a hold-up at customs, so by the time her group of guests were assembled in the coach they were all tired, tempers were short and there were many complaints, often about things over which she had absolutely no control.

'There was no food on the flight,' moaned Mrs Garfield, an extremely overweight woman, with a drooping mouth and a sagging body. She looked like nothing so much as a bad-tempered pug-dog, her flattened face in a permanent discontented sneer.

'You were served with a snack, I'm sure,' said Karen, 'as promised in the brochure.'

Mrs Garfield sniffed. 'Coffee and biscuits. What good is that?'

Karen allowed herself one second's smile as she visualised Mrs Garfield on skis, before turning to deal with the next problem.

'My skis haven't arrived,' said a man, bearing down on Karen angrily. 'They seem to have been left in London or put on the wrong flight.'

'Don't worry, sir, I'll check with London as soon as I can,' said Karen soothingly, 'and in the meantime we can certainly supply you with replacement skis. You won't miss a moment on the slopes.'

'Is there any snow?' The question came from a girl of about sixteen.

'Yes, plenty,' smiled Karen, 'it's beautiful.'

The girl seemed inclined to ask further questions but the woman with whom she was travelling hushed her.

'Karen is too busy to answer questions now, Charlotte.'

The girl, Charlotte, pouted sulkily. 'I only wanted to know what the skiing was like, Aunt. She's supposed to answer questions about the resort. That's her job!'

She glared at Karen who had passed by to speak to another couple further up the coach.

'Certainly she is, but not when she's run off her feet and we're behindhand already.'

Karen mentally blessed the thoughtful aunt and continued checking off names on her list. At last, all the guests and their luggage were loaded and the coach rumbled into the darkness to negotiate the hairpin bends leading up to St Wilhelm.

After she had given a brief introductory chat about St Wilhelm, most of her clients slept for the rest of the journey and Karen was able to go over which name fitted which face.

Some were not easily forgotten: grumbling pug-faced Mrs Garfield and her hen-pecked husband, Mr Short whose skis were in London, Miss Charlotte Armstrong and her aunt, Miss Emma Armstrong, but Karen prided herself on her memory for names and faces and reckoned she could learn them all in a day.

When they arrived at the Hotel Adler, everyone tumbled out of the stuffy coach and gasped at the sharpness of the night mountain air.

Clutching suitcases and skis, bags and boots, they trailed up the steps and into the hotel lobby. Karl was there to make them welcome, wearing his 'workaday' smile. It did not take long to sort out which guests had which rooms and, apart from Mrs Garfield, who did not like her room, because it looked to the east and the early sun would wake her, all seemed satisfied. A cold buffet was laid out in the dining-room, as they had arrived too late for dinner, and soon everyone was eating well and feeling better for it.

Karen had found a letter waiting on her return and recognised Marianne's writing on the envelope. As she snatched a meal, she allowed herself a moment to read it. Marianna wrote of family news, Helen's dancing classes, Ken's promotion, and tucked into the envelope was a tiny sprig of mistletoe.

'The enclosed is for your own private use,' wrote Marianne, 'and make sure you use it, several times! We'll miss you at Christmas, but know you'll be very busy and enjoying yourself with all that super skiing.

Lucky girl. Do write soon and tell us all about it.'

Karen held the mistletoe against her cheek for a moment and then dropped it back into the envelope. Not much chance of using it here, but the guests would probably enjoy it; she would put it up for them.

Karl met Karen in the hall briefly after supper and said, 'You look tired. How did it go?'

Karen smiled wanly. 'I'll be glad to get to bed,' she admitted. 'It was all right, usual bunch.'

They were interrupted by Charlotte Armstrong, who sauntered over and broke into their conversation without consideration.

'Is there a disco in this place?'

Karl turned politely to reply, though if he had realised then the trouble she was going to cause during her stay he might well have answered her in a different tone.

'There's not one in this hotel, though we do offer live music several nights of the week. There is one just across the square, called 'The Drop Inn'.'

'How do I find it?' demanded Charlotte, who had changed from the rather creased trouser-suit in which she had arrived, and was now devastating in a pink blouse and tight blue denim jeans, both of which emphasised every maturing curve in her body. Her pale hair was swept back in a careless pony-tail and knotted with a pink scarf and her black half-boots nearly tipped her over, their heels were so high.

'I'll show you,' said a voice and Hans-Peter, who had just walked in the door with Marta, stepped forward, his smile devoted entirely to Charlotte.

'Who are you?' said Charlotte, obviously not unaffected by the attention of the handsome young man.

'Hans-Peter at your service.' He was wearing his most charming smile and his moody eyes smouldered under drooping lids. Charlotte tossed her head, ignoring Marta entirely, and said, 'So, show me.'

'Sure,' said Hans-Peter. 'You don't have to be back at any special time, do you?'

'No, of course not.'

Charlotte sent a scornful glance across to her aunt, who was drinking coffee in the lounge.

'I come and go as I choose. My father's Sir David Armstrong!'

'Great,' said Hans-Peter, simply, 'let's go.'

And they went, leaving poor Marta standing open-mouthed at the speed with which she had been ditched and replaced. She had not understood much of the exchange, which had been in English, but she certainly understood what had happened. She turned on her father.

'That's your fault,' she burst out. 'If you didn't make me come in at half-past ten that would never have happened!'

And she pushed past him and ran upstairs sobbing.

Karl strode to the bottom of the

stairs and called up after her angrily, but she had gone and the slamming of a door showed she was not coming down again.

'Shall I go and talk to her?' asked Karen, impulsively putting a hand on Karl's arm.

He pulled away.

'You'll not interfere,' he snapped. 'This is a family matter,' and he turned on his heel and disappeared into his office.

Karen felt as if he had slapped her face in public. Hiding her humiliation in forced cheerfulness, she went to see that all her guests were content, then instead of going to bed as she had planned she crossed the square to Johann's bar.

5

It was a bitterly cold night, so that Karen shivered in spite of her warm ski-suit, fur boots and gloves. A half-moon, pale and cold, sailed in the charcoal sky, making the smooth wide slopes above the village gleam with a strange, supernatural phosphorescence. The jutting peaks of the mountains were lost in the darkness, nothing more than dark shadows against a darker sky.

The crisp snow on the ground crunched beneath Karen's feet — the only sound in the still square asleep beneath its blanket of snow — and her breath exploded into angry clouds as she walked briskly towards Johann's.

The square was deserted and Karen paused for a moment in front of Rudi Meyer's sports shop's lighted window, gazing at the displayed boots, skis and ski-suits and thinking of the next morning when many of her guests would be crowding in there to hire the equipment they needed.

A little calmer now, she walked on more slowly, but there was still the flush of anger in her cheeks, heightened by the cold night air and her eyes sparkled with fury as she remembered Karl's words and the way he had humiliated her in full view of the guests.

'How dare he?' she fumed. 'How dare he? I was only trying to help.'

Karen was glad that she had somewhere to go, somewhere she knew she would be welcome. She longed to pour out what happened to someone sympathetic. If only Marianne were within reach, just to listen while Karen exploded the bottled-up anger out of her system. Donald Keary had been right, there were going to be occasions when she was lonely and felt cut off from all her friends, and this was one of them. Perhaps she would talk to Johann, after all she had told him about Roger and found him a good listener;

perhaps that was why she had automatically turned her steps that way now; all she knew was that she had to get away from the Hotel Adler for a while.

As she pushed open the door, the warmth in the bar engulfed her, flooding round her, such warmth sharply contrasting with the bitter cold outside. She paused inside, surprised to find the place almost empty, then Johann greeted her, calling her name across the bar and smiling she went to join him.

'Well, this is a surprise,' he said cheerfully, 'I didn't expect to see you tonight. Thought you'd be up to your eyes in guests and lost passports.'

Karen laughed.

'Lost skis actually, but I think it's all under control now, so I thought I'd come over for a glass of fresh orange juice, I reckon I've earned one.'

She glanced round the almost empty bar; only one table was occupied and the deserted tables and fireside settles looked rather forlorn.

'Where is everyone?' she asked.

'We're quiet tonight,' answered Johann with a shrug as he prepared and poured her usual glass of fresh orange.

'I thought the whole place would be swinging.'

Johann laughed. 'I'm here, you're here, what else is needed to swing?'

He paused and looked at her hard.

'What's the matter? You look uptight about something. Is there anything wrong?'

Karen smiled tiredly. 'Nothing much. I had a bit of an argument with Karl this evening, that's all.'

'Oh, what was that about then?'

Now was her opportunity to give vent to her rage, but somehow in spite of Johann's sympathetic interest she found she no longer wanted to tell him. Something held her back, perhaps it was the triviality of the whole affair, or was it the knowledge that she had been hurt by such a trivial incident? Karl Braun was not important to her and Johann should not be allowed to think he was.

She sipped her drink and said as casually as she could, 'Really, it was nothing much, but I was annoyed at the time and thought a change of scene would do me good, so here I am.'

'So, here you are,' agreed Johann, 'and I'm delighted to see you. Come on, you need to relax, let's go and sit over there by the stove and you can tell me your troubles.'

Johann carried the drinks over and set them on the table, Karen took off her ski-jacket and flopped on to an old wooden settle beside the stove. She sighed. 'I don't know why I'm so tired,' she said. 'It's getting back to the old routine, I suppose,' and she told Johann about her journey from the airport and the clients she had collected.

'Any beautiful young ladies?' asked Johann hopefully. Karen laughed. 'Yes, but you're too late. Your Hans-Peter has gone off with the best. Poor Marta is very upset.'

'Oh, I'll soon cut him out,' grinned Johann. 'What appeal can a young boy have compared with a mature man of experience? Then Marta can have Hans-Peter back again.'

They both laughed and Karen felt better. Without giving a graphic account of what had happened, she had alluded to the incident, if only in passing, and suddenly she found it had slipped back into proportion. She glanced at the other couple, sitting heads together in a corner of the bar.

'What about your other customers?'

'Well, they're hardly going to get killed in the rush to the bar, are they?' Johann grinned ruefully. 'When are you going to bring your lot in? I can organize a Tyrolean evening if you like.'

'But that's being held over at the Adler,' said Karen in surprise.

'Well, I can have one too, can't I?' Johann sounded irritated. 'And you can bring your lot to mine.'

'Oh, Johann, I can't. You know I can't alter it now.' Karen was a little surprised at his attitude. Johann must realise she couldn't simply walk out on an evening that had been arranged expressly for the benefit of her clients.

'Karl Braun and I arranged it when I first arrived. It's going to be a weekly event down in the keller-bar. I'm sorry, Johann, I can't go back on that. We're already coming here for a 'Sociable Evening at Johann's' on Friday, aren't we? They'll love it in here, I'm sure, especially if they could meet up with their ski-instructors as well as some other local people. Could you get them to come?'

'Well, we give the medals from the ski-school races on Friday evenings. I was planning to do that at the same time.'

'There you are then,' said Karen, relieved. 'All my guests will have to come to find out their times and collect their medals and the instructors will be here to collect a drink from their winning pupils.'

'You're right, of course. That'll be fine then.'

Johann looked more cheerful again, but Karen felt suddenly drained. She had come over here to escape her work for an hour and found herself involved with it again and the next day loomed large in her mind.

'I must go,' she said, picking up her jacket. 'Thanks for the drink and sympathy.'

'Anytime,' said Johann, heartily, now entirely his usual self again.

'See you tomorrow, I expect. I'm looking forward to meeting your brood, Mother Hen. Now, remember, don't let Karl rile you. You have your job to do and you only have to work with him, he can't tell you what to do. Don't let him bully you.'

'I won't,' promised Karen. 'Thanks again. I'm glad I came,' and impulsively she reached up and kissed his cheek.

'So am I,' said Johann, returning her kiss with enthusiasm. 'I'm always here and you're always welcome.'

'I'll remember,' said Karen. 'Good-night,' and she left the friendly warmth of the bar for the cold outside and the Adler hotel.

It was later than she had thought and when Karen had crossed the square and pushed open the heavy front doors of the Hotel Adler she found that the main hall was only dimly lit by two small lamps and the lounge and the bar were in darkness. Obviously all the guests had gone to bed and Karen paused, wondering if the front door should be locked; she had never come in this late before. Then she noticed a gleam of light beneath the office door and, realising Karl Braun must still be up and would see to his own locking up, she started towards the stairs.

As she crossed the hall, however, the office door opened and Karl appeared, silhouetted in the doorway.

'Ah, Fräulein Miller, you're back. I was beginning to worry about you.' He spoke smoothly, with no signs of his supposed worry.

Karen kept a tight hold on her temper. 'Don't let him rile you,' Johann had said, 'you only have to work with him, don't let him bully you.'

'I'm sorry if I kept you up,' she answered stiffly. 'I should have told you I'd be in late.'

'It doesn't matter, I was working in any case. Besides, that little madam in the blue jeans isn't in yet.'

His face hardened as he mentioned Charlotte Armstrong. Then he continued, 'However, as I have seen you I would like to apologise for speaking to you as I did earlier. I know you meant well and I didn't mean to be rude; it's just that I was so angry with that stupid little girl.'

'With Marta?' Karen was startled.

'No, no, not Marta, though I might well be cross with her too. No, that Armstrong girl. Will you join me for a nightcap?'

The change of subject was so sudden that it took Karen unawares. She was about to say that she was going to bed but decided it sounded ungracious after his apology, so she said, 'Thank you. Just a quick one.'

He led the way into his office and,

taking two glasses from a corner-table, poured a large measure of brandy into each. He held one glass up to the light and then passed it beneath his nose, inhaling gently.

'This is a really excellent brandy,' he said, handing the other glass to Karen and waving her into one of the two armchairs. 'I treat myself from time to time, to celebrate or to cheer myself up.'

Karen looked round the office. She had been in it several times, but now somehow it looked different, less official, more of a private study than an office. The desk-top was littered with work as always, but there was something homely about the deep armchairs, the room mellow in the lamplight and the curtains drawn against the cold outside.

She sat in the chair, her feet drawn up, comfortably beneath her, nursing her brandy. She sipped it and felt the fire of it travel down through her.

'Which was it this time?' she enquired.

'Cheering up,' said Karl. 'I hate to see Marta hurt and she's going to be with that Armstrong girl about. If she were mine . . . '

'If she were yours,' remarked Karen, 'she wouldn't behave like that.' She ignored Karl's quick glance and continued, 'I'm almost certain she's the daughter of Sir David Armstrong, who's a leading industrialist in England. She's been thoroughly spoilt as her parents only spend money on her, not time with her. Expensive boarding-school and trips abroad, instead of a nice comfortable home background and family atmosphere.'

'You seem to know a lot about her,' smiled Karl. 'Do you research all your clients like that?'

'Of course not,' Karen spoke sharply, 'but he's been in the news a great deal lately and I read a feature article about him just before I left England.'

'What's he been doing that's so newsworthy?' asked Karl, settling himself back into his chair and stretching out his long legs comfortably in front of him. 'Why the article?'

'His firm has been on strike and it has lasted a very long time. They were very close to a settlement and then for some reason it all went wrong. Anyway, in the end there was a lock-out and all his factories are closed. It's created a terrible situation and no one knows where they all go from here.'

'And this is the daughter?'

'I think so, from what she said and what I could gather from talking with her aunt, the one she's travelling with. They're here for three weeks, which is unusual — even over the Christmas period. I think she must be spending her entire school holidays here.'

'Hmm, that's a pity,' said Karl, 'especially if she flaunts Hans-Peter under Marta's nose all the time.'

'Which she will,' promised Karen. 'Possessions are all she has and she'll regard Hans-Peter as one for as long as she's interested in him.'

Silence drifted through the room like

a mountain mist; surrounding both Karl and Karen so that each lapsed into his or her private world. Karen found herself studying Karl as he gazed into his brandy-glass.

He was as different from the daytime Karl as the room was different. He was relaxed and at ease, comfortable in the friendly familiarity of his study. The lines of worry were smoothed from his face and suddenly he looked younger. Karen wondered about his age; he must be about thirty-eight, she decided, not old at all. He glanced up from his meditation and, catching her gaze, smiled. Karen felt confused and, downing the last of her brandy in one draught of fire, she jumped to her feet.

'I must go to bed,' she said, as she set the glass on the table. 'It's going to be one hell of a day tomorrow, getting everyone organised with their equipment and things. Thanks for the brandy, I'll see you in the morning.'

Karl's formality returned and he

stood up too. 'Yes, of course. Goodnight.'

Karen crossed the hall but was halted at the foot of the stairs by Karl, from the door of his office. 'And keep that Armstrong girl out of Marta's way.'

His voice seemed hard once more and Karen felt her face tense. 'I'll try, Herr Braun, but I can't promise.'

The office door closed and Karen was left standing at the foot of the stairs in the dimly lit hall. She felt strangely alone as she went up to bed and almost wondered if the strange brief interlude had happened at all.

6

After breakfast next morning, Karen gathered her guests together in the lounge and explained about the skiing.

Most of them had hired equipment to collect and she sent them off to Rudi Meyer to try on boots and select skis, those with their own skis and boots were anxious to get out on the snow and she sent those off to the lift company's office near the cable-car to collect the lift passes which allowed them use of all the lifts in the area.

There were surprisingly few problems at first and they were easily dealt with. Mr and Mrs Drew, a young couple on their second skiing holiday, had forgotten to bring photographs for their lift passes, so Karen had to send them off to the photographer in the village.

'I'm afraid it will cost more here,' she

said, 'but he'll do it very quickly for you.'

She was just explaining how to find the way to Gunter Klaus's studio, when Marta appeared. Karen explained their problem and Marta was quick to offer her help.

'I'll take them, Karen,' she said, 'and I can interpret for them when we get there. I was going to come and help you at Rudi's, but I'll join you there later. You'll be there for some time, I expect.'

She turned to the Drews and said slowly in English, 'I will show you the house of Gunter Klaus. I know him for much years and I will talk with him for you.'

The Drews were delighted and all three set off to find Gunter Klaus.

Mr Short had to be supplied with skis until his own arrived next day and so Karen took him to Rudi Meyer and explained the situation.

Rudi Meyer's shop was crowded and hot. Rudi's wife, Frieda, was bustling here and there trying to fit everyone with ski-boots, while her husband and son were sorting out skis and sticks and adjusting the bindings of the chosen skis to fit the chosen boots.

Rudi saw Karen come in and raised his hand in brief salute. Leaving his son, Franz, with the skis, he came over.

'It's been chaotic in here this morning,' he grinned, 'but very good for business, so we don't complain, eh?'

Karen said she'd love to lend a hand and asked him to suit Mr Short with some good skis.

'Write the ticket and I'll sign for them,' she said.

Rudi agreed and Karen went to the assistance of some of her guests who had never seen ski-boots before and had no idea how the clips worked or how the boots should feel when they are on. Mrs Garfield sat struggling with a pair on a chair in a corner. Karen went over to her.

'Can I help you with those?'

'I don't know,' Mrs Garfield grumbled, 'I asked that girl for size six and she brought these. These can't be sixes, look how much longer than my shoes they are. It doesn't say six on them anywhere.'

'It won't, Mrs Garfield, because they're continental sizes and they look long because of the extra pieces back and front. That's where the skis clip on. Don't worry, we'll get you into them and I'll show you how to do them up. Have you brought a ski-sock with you like I said? Right, well put it on and we'll try on the boots.'

Karen spent sometime fitting boots and answering questions, but at last everyone seemed to be satisfied with what they had got and Karen felt in need of a coffee. It was then that Charlotte made her entrance and entrance it was, carefully planned to create the biggest sensation and attract the most attention. She marched into the shop and pausing in the doorway announced in a shrill carrying voice, 'I wish to see the owner. Fetch him here.'

It was her words which caused

everyone to look up, but it was not her words which made them all continue to stare, it was her outfit.

She was dressed in a ski-suit, the jacket of which stopped short above her waist, nipped in to emphasise its slimness and the slight swell of her hips. It was a shimmering silver powdered with tiny golden stars, across the front was a sunburst in gold and when she stepped forward Karen could see the curve of a golden crescent moon across the back. To complete the outfit, Charlotte was wearing knee-length après-ski boots of soft white fur and a fur hat. It was outrageous and she looked stunning. Karen had certainly never seen a suit like it before. As if in answer to her unspoken thought, Charlotte said to the shop in general, 'Do you like my suit? My father, Sir David Armstrong, had it made especially for me. I designed it myself. Now, where is the owner or manager or someone in charge?'

Karen was glad Marta had gone with the Drews to the photographer, and not come to help Karen in the ski-shop, as originally planned. Karen could only guess at her reaction to the vision which had just walked in and it was not a consoling thought.

'Now, Miss Armstrong,' said Karen, coming forward, 'let's see if we can find some boots your size.'

'I have boots,' said Charlotte, turning to Karen disdainfully, 'I have come for skis. My father told me to get the best, so what have you got?'

Her question was directed at Rudi, who had come across to see what she wanted.

'You want to buy skis or hire them?' asked Karen, a little at a loss by the turn events were taking.

'To buy them, of course. What have you got?'

At that moment, the shop door opened and Charlotte's aunt came in carrying a pair of silver ski-boots.

'Ah, there you are, dear. I think you'll need your boots when you're buying your skis.'

The arrival of Miss Emma Armstrong somehow brought a feeling of normality back to the shop and everyone turned back reluctantly to what they had been doing.

Karen left aunt and niece in the capable hands of Rudi and his wife and shepherded her group of beginners out into the square, laden with skis and boots.

The morning glistened round them, the sun in a cloudless blue sky sparkled on the snow-covered houses and struck fire from the long stilettos of ice which festooned the eaves and window-sills.

Karen longed to ride the lift to the top of one of the snowy peaks above the village and then ski downward again with the freedom of a bird, curving her way across the magnificence of the mountains, alone with their grandeur.

'Karen, what do we do now?' asked one of the group waiting.

Reluctantly, she drew her mind back to reality and promising herself at least one decent run this afternoon when all her guests were safely in ski-school or exploring the mountain themselves; she gave her clients her attention now.

'Ski-school starts at 1.30,' she told them. 'I'll meet you at the hotel and take you to the ski-school meeting-place then. In the meantime there is a nursery slope at the back of the hotel.'

She laughed at the horror on some of the faces round her.

'Don't panic, it's not steep, but you might like to try your skis by yourselves before lessons start, particularly if any of you have taken dry-ski instruction at home.'

'We did,' said two girls who Karen knew were travelling together.

'Well, have a go then,' said Karen. 'You'll find it very much easier on snow than on those nylon brushes.'

Seeing Marta crossing the square towards Rudi Meyer's shop, Karen said hastily, 'I'll see you all after lunch,' and slipped away to catch Marta before she went into the shop and saw Charlotte.

'Hey, Marta,' she called, 'did you sort

the Drews out all right?'

Marta waved a cheerful hand. 'Yes,' she called.

'Then let's go and have a coffee somewhere.'

Marta stopped and turned back.

'Gunter Klaus did the photos,' she said. 'Those people are getting their passes now.'

'Good. Let's go and have a coffee. I feel I've earned it.'

Karen linked her arm through Marta's and drew her away from Rudi's shop.

'We could go to Johann's,' said Marta hopefully.

'So we could,' agreed Karen, perfectly aware of why Marta wanted to go there and hoping that Hans-Peter, if he were there, would pay the girl some attention.

They turned into the little alleyway and wandered down to Johann's. The little bar was open, but empty; it always seemed strangely dark and deserted during the daytime Karen thought, not really very welcoming at all, though it was beautifully warm when you came in from the outside. Perhaps it was because the alley itself was dimmed by the overhanging roofs and little light came in through the windows, even on the sunniest day. At night, with the lights and the music, it seemed much more cheerful. Karen hoped the Friday evenings there would be a success.

Johann heard the door close and came through from the back room. He shouted when he saw who it was.

'Well, this is nice,' he said. 'Two beautiful ladies appearing to brighten my morning.'

'We're customers today,' announced Marta. 'We want two cups of coffee and two apple strudels.' Karen began to protest that coffee was all she wanted, but Johann was already selecting two delicious pieces of apple strudel and putting them on plates.

'Business is a little slow today,' he said, as he settled them at a table near the stove, 'you must recommend me to all your guests, Karen, suggest they come here for their mid-morning coffee.'

'I did tell them about you this morning,' said Karen. She wished Johann would leave the subject of her guests and his bar alone for a while; however she merely said, 'And they're coming on Thursday evening, at least some of them are, I think — you must take it from there yourself. Once they've been, they're sure to come back, especially if you do the ski-school party.'

As they were drinking their coffee, Karen was conscious of Marta's continually looking past her to the door behind the bar.

'Where's Hans-Peter this morning?' Karen asked Johann casually, hoping to put the girl out of her misery.

'He's going out this morning, said he'd arranged to meet someone.' Johann smiled at Marta. 'I thought it was you; have you come to see him? He's teaching this afternoon.'

'No, no,' exclaimed Marta hastily, 'I'm helping Karen this morning — with her guests.'

Suddenly the back-room door opened and Hans-Peter appeared. Without even looking at Marta, he said to Johann, 'I'll see you at the ski-school at half past one.'

'Well, don't be late,' replied Johann, 'we're always busiest the first session, sorting everyone out.'

'Good-morning, Hans-Peter,' said Karen, pointedly. He had the grace to look embarrassed and, turning to the two women, he made a formal little bow, saying stiffly, 'Good-morning.' Then with a quick 'See you later, Johann' he made his escape to the street.

After one look at Marta's face, Johann made a discreet withdrawal behind the bar, leaving Karen to cope with Marta.

'You mustn't let that silly boy's behaviour upset you, you know,' Karen said, handing Marta a handkerchief and inwardly cursing Hans-Peter.

'He may be only nineteen,' she thought, 'but he should take more care of other people's feelings.'

How was she going to warn Marta about Charlotte? — but Marta did not need any warning.

'He's gone to meet that English girl.'

Marta's voice was flat and unemotional and, glancing at her, Karen saw that she had dried her eyes. She decided that the only approach was the honest and direct one.

'Yes, you're right,' she said. 'Charlotte Armstrong came into Rudi's just now, to buy some skis.'

'To buy?' Marta was amazed. 'Can she ski?'

'I don't know,' admitted Karen, 'but I think probably not. She's got all the gear though and is out to make a big impression all round, not only on Hans-Peter. She's that sort of girl, Marta, but she won't be here forever.'

'Nor will Hans-Peter,' wailed Marta. 'He'll go back to university and I'll never see him again.' The tears began to stream down her face again.

Karen leaned across the table and took Marta's hands in hers.

'Now listen, Marta; I know you're fond of Hans-Peter and you don't want to hear about the other fish in the sea, but you mustn't ruin your Christmas holiday by being miserable over him. He's not worth it. It's up to you to help make Christmas and New Year a happy time, especially at the hotel. I'm going to need all the help I can get.'

She supplied Marta with a second handkerchief and went on, 'You were great to cope with the Drews this morning, I'd probably still be at Rudi's now if I'd had to go to Gunter Klaus's as well. And your father and grandmother will need your help too.'

Marta pouted. 'Daddy doesn't understand. He thinks I'm still a baby — he doesn't realise I'm grown up.'

Karen smiled. 'Most fathers think that you know. My father treated me as a little girl until the day he died! But your father loves you dearly and he doesn't want to see you hurt.'

Karen paused, not knowing quite how much to say. If Karl could hear her he would certainly accuse her of interfering in a private family matter, but on the other hand Karen felt that Marta needed someone to talk to. Perhaps she should say no more, leave it to Frau Leiter to help the girl through her first heartbreak; on the other hand, Marta seemed more ready to talk to her, Karen, than her grandmother.

'You must show your father that you're grown up enough to cope with silly young men, like Hans-Peter.'

'He's not silly.' Marta rushed to Hans-Peter's defence.

'Well, he's let himself be bowled over by a pretty face and a lot of surface glitter.'

'Surface glitter?'

'Yes.' Karen allowed herself a laugh. 'Oh, Marta, you should see her ski-suit. She designed it herself. It's all suns and moons and stars.'

Marta did not return Karen's laugh.

'I suppose she looked fantastic.'

'Well, she did,' admitted Karen, 'but I bet her skiing doesn't keep up with her suit. You'll leave her standing there.' Karen ventured another laugh. 'Or sitting on her bottom in the snow.'

Marta managed a weak smile.

'That's better. Don't give either Hans-Peter or Charlotte the satisfaction of seeing you're upset. Keep your pride.'

'Fine advice coming from you,' Karen thought to herself, 'after the way you trampled your own pride over Roger.'

'I know it's not easy — believe me, I know,' and quietly Karen told Marta about Roger and her own misery when her engagement broke up.

And Marta listened, forgetting for the present anyway her own heartache as her sympathy and indignation grew on Karen's behalf.

'So, I've come right away and am very involved in my work,' concluded

Karen. 'And it seems to be working,' she thought privately, because she suddenly realised that the old familiar dull ache when she thought of Roger was no longer there. She had told Marta the whole story with scarcely a twinge. Her pride still hurt a little she realised as she noted the pity in the younger girl's eyes, but the desolate empty space within her seemed to have gone.

'I'm so busy, I haven't room in my life for emptiness,' she decided and then realised that while she had been examining her own reactions Marta had been speaking to her.

'Sorry, I was miles away for a minute. What did you say?'

'I said,' repeated Marta, a little petulantly, 'that I can't get away like that.'

'No,' agreed Karen, 'but you can get involved in all the Christmas preparations and you can ski whenever you feel like it — you're lucky because you've plenty to do and you've always got me for a chat when you're feeling low.'

She rose to her feet and reached for her jacket.

'Come on,' she said, 'I must get back and do some paperwork. I've promised myself an hour's skiing this afternoon.'

'Can I come too?' asked Marta eagerly.

Karen would have much preferred to have skied alone, but, seeing the hopeful look on Marta's face, she hadn't the heart to refuse her.

'Of course,' she said. 'On two conditions: one is that you don't let your feelings show to Charlotte or Hans-Peter and the other is that you really give a hand at home, with all the decorating and things.'

Marta nodded her agreement and, saying goodbye to Johann, they left the bar and went out into the dazzling sunlight in the square.

'We're decorating tomorrow,' said Marta, as they wandered back to the hotel. 'I heard Daddy tell Oma that they'd be getting the greenery tomorrow.'

'I've got a little something to add to the decorations actually,' said Karen and she explained about the mistletoe Marianne had sent her.

'What a lovely idea,' cried Marta. 'We must remember to put it up.'

When they reached the hotel, the guests were assembling for lunch, some in the bar and others already in the dining-room. As they came in through the door, Karl stepped out of his office.

'Ah, there you are,' he said. 'Successful morning?'

'Yes, thank you,' said Karen. 'Everyone seems to be organised now I think and when they're all in ski-school this afternoon I shall be able to relax a little.'

'I will too,' said Karl and, turning to Marta, he added, 'I thought we might ski this afternoon, Marta, we haven't been out together for a long time.'

'Oh, sorry, Dad,' said Marta. 'I'm already going with Karen. I promised ages ago to show her all the runs.'

'I'm sure she'll excuse you this time,'

Karl said smoothly, leaving Karen in no doubt that his invitation was almost a command.

'Well . . . ' Marta hesitated. Then she brightened. 'We could all go together, couldn't we? That would be fun. Karen's an awfully good skier, you know, we'd have a marvellous time.'

'Some other time perhaps,' said Karl. 'Today I'd like you to myself. I'm sure Karen will understand.'

'Of course,' said Karen. 'I'll see you later,' and she turned away and went up to her room.

She dropped into her chair and gazed out across the village to the mountains beyond. The sun was still bright and the snow crisp and inviting, but somehow in some ridiculous way Karen felt left out.

She had been longing to be alone up on the slopes, to escape and explore and the thought of Marta's coming with her had taken the edge off her anticipated enjoyment; now the fact that Karl and Marta were not including her in their afternoon out and she was able to revert to her original plan of skiing alone, perversely made her look forward to her afternoon even less.

'Some people are never satisfied,' she thought and, giving herself a mental shake, she tried to put everything out of her mind as she turned to the paperwork which littered her table.

7

The ski-school meeting-place was near the bottom station of the chairlift, a wide flat area with marker-posts indicating where each group should stand according to the skiing experience of its members. The sun shone down from a cloudless, pale blue sky and there was a feeling of barely suppressed excitement amongst the skiers assembled there, stamping their feet, blowing on their hands and recounting, amidst gales of laughter, stories of the morning's excitement on the slopes.

Karen's guests from the Hotel Adler had been joined by several Germans and a party of Dutch who were staying at the little guest houses about the village and the numbers were still further swollen by the arrival of two buses from Feldkirch and one from Rheindorf, the two sister villages around the mountain. Chattering skiers tumbled out to join the crowd adding to the confusion as they milled round collecting skis from the racks on the backs of the buses. Karen stayed with her group of beginners waiting a little apprehensively for the arrival of their instructor.

'He will be able to speak English, won't he?' asked Mrs Garfield. 'I don't want to go with a man who can only talk German.'

'Don't worry, Johann, the ski-school director knows this group is English and he's certain to choose an instructor who can teach in English.' Karen turned to the two girls, Carolyn and Julie, who had had some lessons at home. 'Did you have a try this morning?'

'Oh yes, it was great fun,' said Julie laughing. 'We sat down quite a bit, but I did remember how to snow-plough.'

'Good,' said Karen, 'it's only a matter of confidence and you'll find . . . ' but she was interrupted by the arrival of

Charlotte Armstrong, who with her usual lack of courtesy marched up to Karen and throwing down the brand-new skis and sticks she was carrying demanded, 'Put my skis on for me, Karen, I can't remember how that man said the clamps worked.'

'Bindings,' corrected Karen. 'The metal pieces that hold your boots to the skis are called bindings.'

'Well, anyway,' went on Charlotte with an imperious wave of her hand, 'show me what I do.'

Charlotte's arrival had caused quite a stir in the surrounding group. She was made immediately conspicuous by the unique design of her ski-suit and her voice had that carrying quality usually associated with town criers. There were several admiring glances and Karen had to admit the girl did look stunning, but she did wish that Charlotte did not always dominate any group she was in.

'Like this,' Karen explained quietly, kneeling down in the snow and guiding Charlotte's feet, resplendent in their silver ski-boots, into the bindings of her gleaming skis.

'Now, stamp down and they will automatically close round the toe and heel of your boot.' Charlotte did as she was told and found her feet firmly attached to her skis.

'You chose beautiful skis,' said Karen admiringly. 'You should learn quickly on those.'

'Yes, Hans-Peter said they were good when he saw them this morning,' said Charlotte casually. 'They certainly should be,' she added impressively, 'they cost a fortune, but Daddy said get the best, so I have. The trouble with hired skis,' she continued, addressing the company at large and the group round her in particular, 'is that you never know how they've been treated, people take no care of hired equipment.'

Karen was irritated by this comment, especially as nearly all the others who would be in Charlotte's class were on hired skis.

'Then I suggest you treat them better

than you did just then,' she said with asperity. 'Throwing them down like that does the edges no good at all and can be dangerous, particularly if there is any sort of slope, because they slide away remarkably quickly and can injure anyone they hit, or cause an accident.' Charlotte flushed angrily, but before she could speak Karen added, more gently, 'That's why you have those safety-straps round your legs so that when you fall, if you fall awkwardly and your bindings give way and release your boots, your skis stay with you and don't career off down the hill.'

The ski-instructors arrived altogether resplendent in red sweaters and red ski-hats. They stood in a group talking with Johann who then went from group to group asking about ability and experience. He came up to the group round Karen and she was amused to see his eyes open just a fraction wider as they rested on Charlotte.

'Well, Karen, these are beginners, yes?' He spoke in careful English and she answered him in the same language.

'Yes, none of them has skied before except these two,' and she indicated Carolyn and Julie, 'on a dry slope.' Johann nodded.

'I will take this class myself,' he said. 'Wait here, everybody, and I will come to you.'

'I want to go into Hans-Peter's class,' announced Charlotte. Johann glanced at her surprised. 'I beg your pardon?' he said.

'I want to go into Hans-Peter's class,' repeated Charlotte loudly.

'I am sorry,' said Johann, 'but it is not possible if you do not ski before. You are beginner, yes?' Charlotte nodded. 'Then you must be with me,' said Johann. 'I take beginners this week. Hans-Peter has class two. For you it is too difficult.' He turned to go but Charlotte was determined. 'If he can't take my class I won't go in a class. I'll have private lessons.'

Johann turned back to her. 'Miss,' he said, 'there are no instructors for private lessons in the afternoons. In the mornings, yes. If you wish to ski today you ski with me. Tomorrow you may have private lessons — in the morning.' And with that Johann left an extremely angry Charlotte and continued his round of the groups.

'What's all that about? Private lessons?' Karen was startled by Karl's voice right behind her. She turned to find Karl and Marta ready to climb up to the chairlift. Karen explained quickly and saw Marta's smile of satisfaction when she heard Charlotte could not ski with Hans-Peter. There was a clatter of skis and sticks and a burst of laughter behind her and Karen turned quickly to find Charlotte sitting on the ground, red with fury, and two others in the group sitting helplessly on top of her. Everyone else had dissolved into laughter, the loudest hoots coming from Marta, revelling in her rival's discomfort. Charlotte had tried to go after Johann and had crossed her skis. Falling, she had grabbed at the nearest thing to save herself and had merely succeeded in pulling over two other people who were as unsteady in their skis as she was. Karen went to their aid and managed to disentangle their legs and skis and sticks.

'Serves you right,' she heard Marta laugh. 'I hope you spend the rest of the week on your backside.' Charlotte did not understand the remark, but she hated being laughed at and was muttering with rage as Karen hauled her back to her feet.

'Come on Marta,' said her father who was having difficulty not to laugh at the evident discomfort of one of his guests. 'Let's go before the classes start to queue for the lift.'

'Bye, Karen, might see you later,' called Marta, as she and Karl skied over to the lift and climbed the slope to the mounting platform.

At last all her charges were in the safe hands of their instructors and Karen was free to enjoy herself. She crossed to the lift and was lucky enough to get on just before the first of the classes arrived to go up the mountain. As she swung peacefully in her chair above the smooth snow she saw Johann taking his class up the nursery slope; he was making them side-step up the hill, a very tiring exercise for the unfit or novice skier. Charlotte was struggling at the end of the line and echoing Marta's 'serves her right' Karen settled down to forget her work for an hour and to enjoy her freedom. At the middle station she slid off the lift and side-stepped herself up the slope leading to the mounting platform for the second chairlift to take her up to the highest ridge of the mountain. She felt herself relaxing as she gazed out over the magnificent view below, the wide sweeps of snow, some jutting outcrops of rock and lower down the tall still trees draped in white, motionless in the sun. Far above her was the outline of the top station and, in-between, pylons standing like sentinels with arms outstretched, carried the wires of the chairlift up and up.

On reaching the top station she slid out over the snow to look at a map showing all the runs and lifts on the mountain. She planned herself a route skiing down to the bottom of another lift, a drag-lift this time, and going up to a different peak, gradually working her way round the mountain and ending up at the cafe beside the middle station, for a welcome hot chocolate. The weather was perfect, the snow was perfect and Karen spent an hour skiing the slopes and riding the lifts, solitary but content. There were plenty of people about, good skiers swooping down the hillside and novices struggling to stay upright, but Karen was in a world of her own of peace and enjoyment. She had only herself to consider. Occasionally she saw other skiers who might have been Karl and Marta, but she was never near enough to be sure. At last she took her final run down from the top and schussed to a stop outside the cafe at the middle station. There was a wide wooden verandah with tables and benches set to catch the sun, but it was growing cold now as the sun slipped behind the mountain crest and Karen decided to have her drink inside. She found it very crowded and had to shoulder her way to the bar to buy her hot chocolate. She saw someone waving and recognised Hans-Peter squashed in at a table. He had brought his class in for some refreshment and was now the centre of a cheerful group. Karen noticed the Drews among them and went across to find out how they had been doing. 'Karen!' they greeted her in delight. 'Isn't this a marvellous place? Isn't the skiing just great? And Hans-Peter's such a good instructor.' Hans-Peter grinned at this. 'Come on, Karen, come and sit with us. Move up please,' he called along the bench and with a good deal of elbowing and laughing a tiny space was made for Karen on the end. She perched unsteadily, nursing her hot drink and listening to the Drews reliving their afternoon's skiing.

The rest of the group were German or Dutch, but the Drews seemed delighted with everyone.

'It doesn't matter if communications get a bit mixed,' laughed Ann Drew. 'We all laugh in the same language and there's been a fair amount of that this afternoon. I'll be covered in bruises tomorrow.'

'You should hold a biggest-bruise competition, Karen,' cried Paul Drew. 'I'm sure Ann would win, she's always on her bottom in the snow.'

'You should have seen Paul,' cried Ann in mock indignation. 'He slid a good thirty feet straight down the hill flat on his back with his feet in the air. Hans-Peter had to pull him out of a snowdrift.' They all laughed at the recollection.

Karen listened to them all, joining in the laughter, her body gradually absorbing the warmth of the room round her. A cold draught from the door made her glance up to see Karl and Marta coming in. They were both flushed with the fresh air and both laughing as they edged their way to the bar. Marta caught sight of Karen and waved; pulling at her father's sleeve, she pointed to Karen's table, smiling and obviously suggesting that they should join her. Then her face changed, her smile faded and she turned away. She had seen Hans-Peter. He had seen her too.

'There's Marta,' he said, too casually to Karen. 'Is she coming over?'

'I doubt it,' said Karen. 'I don't think she's very pleased to see you just now.'

'Silly girl,' he said airily, 'she takes everything too seriously.' He downed the last of his beer and stood up.

'Come on, everybody,' he said. 'A nice easy run back to the village.' And with a great deal of commotion his class straggled out of the cafe after him. Karen felt she should be back at the hotel before her guests came pouring in so she too finished her drink and went outside to collect her skis. Karl and Marta were sitting with their backs to her engrossed in conversation with other people at their table and did not see her leave.

There was no sun now and the bitter cold leapt from the snow to make her shiver. Quickly putting on her skis she followed the forest trail back down to the village. She considered taking the longer route that she had skied with Karl, but decided as dusk was creeping amongst the trees that she would head directly for home; for the hotel.

Karen had time for a quick shower and had changed into warm trousers and a cowl-necked sweater before most of the guests came trailing into the hotel, tired after their first day. Several of them flopped in the chairs in the little bar and ordered glühwein to warm them as they swapped tales of excitement and laughed at the afternoon's events; but most of them climbed the stairs wearily to soak in hot baths and relax before dinner.

Frau Leiter and Karl were in the main hall when Karen came down and

Frau Leiter immediately drew her into the conversation.

'Karen, my dear,' she said, 'we're going to decorate the hotel tomorrow morning, first thing. It is such a family occasion that we want no one left out — I mean the hotel is the home of us all just now, so, if any of your guests would like to help hang the greenery, please tell them they would be most welcome. Isn't that right, Karl?'

He nodded. 'Of course; though I expect most will prefer to ski as they are here for such a short time.'

'Well, dear,' said Frau Leiter cheerfully, 'that's up to them. Karen shall tell them and then we can all get to work tomorrow,' and with that she bustled back to the kitchen.

'Did you enjoy your afternoon on the mountain?' Karl asked politely.

'Oh yes,' said Karen. 'It was absolutely beautiful and I tried several runs I hadn't done before.'

'I hope you understood why I took Marta away alone this afternoon. I wanted to smooth away any bad feeling left from last night.' Karl smiled ruefully. 'My mother-in-law tells me that I don't do enough with the child. There, even that's wrong — she's not a child any more but a young woman and I must let her have more freedom.'

'Was your afternoon a success?' ventured Karen, encouraged by his explanations.

'I think so. We talked as well as skied and, though she didn't exactly pour out her heart to me, we seemed to be on fairly easy terms. It cheered her up to see young Charlotte at a disadvantage anyway. Where on earth did she get that ski-suit?'

Karen laughed. 'She designed it herself and her dear Daddy had it specially made.'

'Well thank goodness Marta doesn't go in for design,' said Karl. 'I couldn't keep up with that!' He paused, seeming unwilling to turn away, then he said, 'Will you be helping to decorate tomorrow?'

‘I’d love to,’ said Karen. ‘I’m looking forward to it.’

‘Well, I’ll see you later,’ and with that Karl disappeared into his office, leaving Karen standing in the hall, strangely pleased at having been asked personally to join in with the decorating.

8

Next morning nearly all the guests, as Karl had predicted, opted to ski. Even the beginners who had by all accounts spent much of their time sitting in the snow were eager to discover how much if anything they had learnt the day before. One or two, however, decided to wait until the sun had softened the snow's icy crust before venturing out again and there were several non-skiers in the group who joined in willingly with the hotel staff making garlands of ivy and pine. Karl and Fritz, the barman, carried in an enormous Christmas tree and set it up in a tub in the corner of the lounge. Karen was put in charge of decorating the tree with several helpers, while Frau Leiter did the hall and Fritz the bar and Karl oversaw the dining-room and lounge. Marta sat in the kitchen making table decorations for the dining-room, setting a candle in a wreath of ivy and spraying silver and gold on to the leaves so that they sparkled in the flickering candle-light.

Karen took immense care with the Christmas tree, because she knew it was the focal point in the lounge. The decorations were all silver and gold and aided by Miss Emma Armstrong, Mrs Garfield and a Mrs Walker whose husband was an experienced skier but who did not ski herself covered the tree with sparkling tinsel and gossamer threads of soft spidersweb snow.

'Normally there would be clip-on candle-holders and real candles,' explained Karl, 'but because of the fire risk in a hotel we are only allowed to use electric lights.' Perched on top of a tall step-ladder, Karen covered the tree with the long skein of fairy lights, carefully twisting the wire among the branches so that the coloured lights gleamed through the tree's needles and lit the tiny silver balls with unexpected flashes of colour. By the time the skiers returned for lunch the hotel looked beautiful, with the dark green of the branches and garlands offsetting the silver and gold of the decorations and the firelight in the lounge flickering reflected amongst the green.

Frau Leiter was delighted. 'You've all done a marvellous job,' she cried. 'I can't remember when it looked more beautiful.' She took Karl by the arm and pulled him into the dining-room to admire Marta's table arrangements.

'Marta, they're quite lovely, darling,' Karl said and gave his surprised daughter a hug. 'You have done them beautifully, don't you think so, Karen?'

'I do,' said Karen. 'I wish I could do arrangements like that.'

'I've done you a special one,' said Marta and leading Karen to her table showed her a charming decoration incorporating little Christmas roses.

'Oh Marta, that's lovely,' cried Karen. 'Thank you so much.' But Marta was not really listening, she had turned her attention back to her father and said, a little uncertainly, 'I did one for your office, Daddy, if you'd like it.'

'Thank you, Marta, I'd love it,' he answered simply and she took his hand and led him to his office to show him.

The next few days were not particularly eventful as Christmas crept nearer. Karen saw little of Marta, she seemed to have taken Karen's advice and was busy helping her grandmother; she went out a good deal and skied with some of her schoolfriends, but kept well clear of Charlotte Armstrong for where she was Hans-Peter was not far behind. Karen herself escaped each day for an hour to the freedom of the slopes. The wide hillsides under the vast expanse of sky gave her great peace of mind. She found she was able to think, to consider her future without any of the heartache which hitherto had made it impossible to look forward. Not that she was making any plans, for the present she was busy and happy, or at least not unhappy, and when she was alone in the white world above the village she felt no urge to move on. One day as she sped down a twisting run through the trees on the far side of the mountain, she saw a little wooden hut. There was nothing strange in that, there were many such deserted shacks up in the hill, used by the local farmers during the summer months, the only difference was that this one was obviously in use now. There was a smoothed trail to the door and there were logs stacked round the walls almost to roof-level in places. The windows were shuttered and there was no smoke coming from the chimney, but the scent of burning pine hung in the air as if the chimney were still warm from a fire in its hearth. A little intrigued, Karen wondered who used a secret hideaway up in the winter forests, but she saw no one. She continued the run down towards the village and soon joined the usual trail back under the chairlift down to the nursery slopes. Coming to her favourite viewpoint, she paused for breath and to enjoy the expanse below her before she returned to the bustle of the hotel. Behind her there was the swish of skis and Karl appeared beside her. His face creasing into his special smile as he spoke was full of warmth and very attractive. This thought passed through Karen's mind before she had time to grasp it but she was more aware of how strong he looked, the strength of his tall lean figure emphasised by his close-fitting ski-pants and jacket.

'Hello,' he called, 'on your own? I thought you were with Johann.'

'No,' answered Karen, surprised, 'Johann has classes.'

'Well he's not there,' said Karl with a shrug. 'Someone said he'd gone off with a friend, I assumed it was you.'

'No, not me.' Karen wondered why he had assumed it, but did not ask.

'Are you going down now?' asked Karl.

'Yes, I'm afraid so,' smiled Karen. 'I must get back and see about the Tyrolean evening tonight.'

'And so must I — for the same reason,' said Karl and made as if to lead the way down.

'Herr Braun,' said Karen staying him for a moment, 'whose is that little cabin up in the forests over to the west?'

'Johann's,' came the reply, 'if you mean the one further up the Schwartzberg trail.'

'Yes, that's the one. Does he use it in the winter?'

'I don't know — you'd better ask him. Are you coming or not?' and with a smile at this brusque invitation Karen followed Karl down to the hotel and the Tyrolean evening.

The planned entertainments had been running fairly smoothly and seemed popular with clients. The Tyrolean evening was held in the hotel's keller-bar and they were entertained by the town's band and a troup of local dancers dressed in the traditional 'lederhosen'. Many of the guests were coaxed into joining in the dances and amidst tremendous hilarity the groups and couples began to coalesce and regroup so that everyone forgot their innate reserve and started to combine into larger groups or split into pairs. Most of the inhibitions about being laughed at had melted away on the slopes and this easiness carried over into the après-ski life.

The social evening at Johann's bar was quite well attended and though it was a much quieter evening generally it did have its high spots. Klaus Werner, one of the ski-instructors, bet Mr Short that he could lift him, sitting in a chair, with only one hand. Klaus was an enormous man and there was suppressed excitement as they all gathered round to see if he could make good his boast. He told Mr Short to sit on one of the straight-backed wooden chairs, then crouching behind him he clasped the chair at the top of one of its back legs and very slowly lifted it in the air twisting his body in the most peculiar contortions to keep the chair from tilting and depositing Mr Short on the floor. With tremendous grunting and groaning he raised the chair until it was at shoulder-height and then with one final heave he hoisted the chair and Mr Short over his head to the cheers of the assembled crowd. He had won his bet and added something to the evening out.

Next morning when Karen had seen all her charges safely on to the hill or out into the village on shopping expeditions, she went towards Johann's bar to see how he thought the previous evening had gone and whether there were any changes he wanted to make for the next. It was a dull morning, the mountain peaks were shrouded in mist and the chairlift vanished into the clouds just above the nursery slope; the air felt clammy, the raw damp penetrating everywhere and Karen hurried to the promised warmth of Johann's bar and a cup of hot coffee. Despite the unpleasant weather the square was crowded as people did their last-minute shopping, for Christmas Eve was next day, and Karen had to stop several times to pass the time of day as she walked the short distance to Johann's. 'It's strange,' she thought, 'how quickly I've become part of this place. It's inevitable in such a small village, I suppose, especially when everyone seems friendly,' but it was a comfortable thought.

She pushed open the door of the bar and found it empty except for Johann, deep in conversation with two men at one of the corner-tables. She paused for a moment on the threshold and then as he did not turn round she crossed the room and put a hand on Johann's shoulder. He leapt to his feet as if she had struck him, spinning round, his face clouded with anger, so that Karen took an involuntary step back. When he saw who it was he passed his hand over his face in an agitated manner as if to remove his angry expression and apologised hastily. 'Karen, I'm so sorry, you startled me. I didn't hear you come in.'

'That's all right,' said Karen, though she felt her heart beating very fast as if she were out of breath — or frightened. As the thought came to her she dismissed it out of hand. What possible reason had she to be frightened of Johann? He was smiling at her now and said in his normal voice, 'I won't be long, Karen, my friends and I have nearly finished our — er — discussion. Hans-Peter!' he called towards the closed connecting door at the back of the bar. The door opened and Hans-Peter peered round it questioningly.

'I've nearly finished here,' said Johann. 'Take Karen through and give her a cup of coffee. I'll be with you in a minute.'

'OK,' said Hans-Peter, 'come through, Karen.'

Karen went into the back room and Hans-Peter had hardly finished making her a coffee when the door opened again and Johann joined them alone.

'Have your friends gone?' asked Karen innocently.

'Yes, they were in hurry.'

'I'm sorry if I made you jump, Johann, you were so deep in conversation.'

'Plotting!' chimed in Hans-Peter laughing.

'Plotting?' laughed Karen. 'What on earth were you plotting?'

'Oh nothing much,' muttered Johann; he turned to Hans-Peter and said, 'Isn't it time you were giving that girl her lesson?'

'Another ten minutes,' said Hans-Peter and ignoring Johann's quelling look added, 'I do think you should warn Karen that she may have competition.'

'Competition?' said Karen in surprise. 'Competition in what?'

'Tour-leading,' said Hans-Peter and, dodging to avoid a cuff aimed at him by Johann, he went out of the door to give Charlotte her private lesson, still laughing.

'Come on, Johann,' said Karen lightly, 'what was all that about?' She settled herself into a chair with her cup of coffee and looked across at him expectantly. Johann looked a little uncomfortable and then said, 'Oh, nothing, it's just that, well, you must realise St Wilhelm is an expanding resort and Lambs aren't the only company interested in coming here. There are others putting out feelers for next year.'

'And they were from one of them?' said Karen. Johann nodded.

'I see. Well it's nice to know when there's opposition about.'

Then, 'How's Charlotte doing these days?' she said lightly, changing the subject. Johann was quick to follow her lead.

'She's progressing quite well actually, the private lessons have been a great success. Hans-Peter's delighted with her — in more ways than one.' He smiled as he said that and the tension eased a little, so they were able to finish their coffee more companionably.

When Karen got back to the privacy of her room she considered what she had learned during her visit to Johann's. There was little doubt Johann had not been going to tell her of the other company interested in moving into St Wilhelm. No doubt they would be approaching Karl about the Hotel Adler — perhaps they had already done so. Karen remembered Donald Keary's warning that Lambs International only had a contract with the hotel for one season and that it was up to her to make it a more permanent arrangement.

'Well,' she thought with determination, 'I won't lose that contract. I'll convince Karl Braun that he's working with an efficient and reliable company. I can do it and I will, even if I have to bite out my tongue to keep on good terms with him.' And she was grateful for the warning Hans-Peter had given her, without considering why Johann would not have alerted her had he not been forced to.

9

Christmas Eve dawned dull and grey with heavy low clouds perched on the mountain peaks, threatening more snow. Mrs Garfield complained loudly to Karen about the lack of sunshine and the uninviting aspect of the nursery slopes outside.

'If I'd wanted to be cold and wet,' she moaned, her pug-face crumpled into a scowl, 'I'd have stayed at home.'

Karen managed a smile although she was finding Mrs Garfield's continual complaints about the food, her room, the attitude of the shopkeepers in the village, her ski-instructor and several other uncontrollable factors of her holiday something of a trial.

'I'm very sorry, Mrs Garfield,' said Karen, 'but I'm afraid control of the weather really is beyond me.'

Mrs Garfield sniffed her displeasure

and, still grumbling, left Karen standing in the hall as she set out to face the grey cold outside.

'Trouble, Karen?' asked Frau Leiter appearing from the kitchen. Karen grinned ruefully. 'No, not really, but some of them do complain about the most ridiculous things and she's the worst.'

'What this time?'

'The weather, as if I could do anything about it. It wasn't just a passing comment like 'no sun again today, I see', but a real complaint.'

Frau Leiter smiled. 'Well, my dear, you're quite right about one thing, you can't do anything about it, so come and have a cup of coffee in the kitchen. There's plenty in the pot and I was going to stop for one myself.' Karen accepted gratefully. She had grown fond of Frau Leiter and found her warm commonsense approach to life very heartening. She followed the old lady into the kitchen and sat down at the big scrubbed table while Frau

Leiter filled two dark blue pottery mugs from an enamelled coffee-pot set beside the stove. Drawing a chair opposite Karen's she passed over one of the mugs and sat nursing the other, her elbows resting on the table. A companionable silence fell and Karen relaxed as she sipped the scalding coffee and felt its warmth flow through her. At length Frau Leiter spoke.

'Well, how's it going? As smoothly as it seems?'

Karen considered for a moment. She had no reason to suspect Frau Leiter of sounding her out directly for Karl and yet somehow from the tone of her voice Karen felt there was more than passing interest in the older woman's question, and her conversation with Johann had put her on her guard. If she answered too confidently it might make Frau Leiter think that she, Karen, felt complacent; on the other hand if she sounded worried that might lead Karl, and she was sure her answer would reach him in the end whether in passing conversation or in deliberate discussion, to think she wasn't able to cope with the job.

'Well,' she replied guardedly, 'it's not been too bad so far. There have been one or two hitches of course, there always will be the unexpected problems, but on the whole I think the arrangements seem to be working out well.'

'Good,' said Frau Leiter. 'I'm glad, because you're an efficient girl and your hard work deserves success. You mustn't worry about people like that Mrs Garfield woman.'

'Oh, I'm not,' said Karen quickly. 'There's always one like her. I remember in Kitzbühel last year there was one man who used to buttonhole me every morning and reel off lists of complaints in a particularly high whining voice. One day a young chap and his girlfriend came up to me and he, imitating that awful voice, said, 'Karen, I've got a complaint to make.' I must say I sighed aloud and said, 'Yes what is it?' then still copying the other man's voice he said, 'Nobody told us it got dark here at night, it really is too bad!' at which we all three burst out laughing; and do you know when the old complainer arrived next day with his list I couldn't stop laughing and he went off in a huff to complain about me to one of the other reps.'

Karen laughed now as she recounted the tale and Frau Leiter laughed too. Then she said, 'But unfortunately for you, Karen, you're the only rep here, there's no one else for Mrs G. to go to.'

Karen nodded. 'I know, but in spite of that and the feeling that one's on duty permanently I'm really enjoying myself. It's hard work, but it's work I like so I don't mind, and the skiing is superb.'

'It's doing you good,' agreed Frau Leiter, getting up to refill the coffee-mugs. 'You look far better than when you first arrived. They say hard work can help to heal an emotional wound.'

Karen looked up sharply. 'What do you mean?'

'I know of the trouble you had before you came. Marta told me about your broken engagement.'

'Well she had no right to do so,' said Karen hotly. 'She was told in confidence. I only told her to help her see that broken hearts can be mended, particularly if it's not much more than bruising.'

'I know, my dear,' soothed Frau Leiter. 'It won't go any further than me; and you must try to forgive Marta. She did not intend to break a confidence, but since her mother died she has really had no one to talk to but me.' Frau Leiter sighed. 'And I'm the wrong generation.' She looked across at Karen. 'You're nearer her age and you certainly helped her the other day when you confided in her. She was proud of your confidence — so proud that she had to tell someone of it; so she told me.' Frau Leiter continued speaking but Karen realised that she was no longer being spoken to directly; Frau Leiter seemed to forget her and was thinking aloud.

'She misses Anna, poor child, more than she realises, I know. I miss her too, my lovely girl. She was so full of life and love. And when she was killed, Karl changed overnight; instead of the loving husband and warm caring man he'd always been, he became harsh and bitter, angry at fate which had so robbed him. Poor Marta, in many ways she lost both her parents the day that Anna died. Karl's accepted it now of course, but he's never quite broken down the protective wall he built round himself. We all need him, but he's never quite there. He loves Marta dearly, I know he does, but he never shows her like he used to do. Perhaps he's afraid. Afraid that he'll lose her too if he shows how much she means to him. The trouble is he'll lose her if he doesn't show her and goes on cutting her out.'

'He skied with her the other day,' said Karen gently as the old lady lapsed into silence. Her voice brought Frau Leiter back to the present.

'Yes, he did and she was very pleased. It was the day she felt people were interested in her again; you and her father. She's still very hurt by that young fool Hans-Peter and I wouldn't put it past her to think of a way to pay him out — or that minx Charlotte Armstrong, but that's still at school-girl level and she's hovering between that and being a woman.' She paused again and looked across at Karen sitting with her untouched second cup of coffee beside her and said gently, 'So don't be angry with her for breaking your confidence.'

'I won't,' said Karen, 'I understand.'

The conversation with Frau Leiter decided her on a point she had been considering for some days now, whether she should give Marta and Frau Leiter small token Christmas presents. She had only known them a few weeks and yet she felt close to them and grateful for the way they had helped her over that time. Now she cut across the square to a little jeweller's opposite the hotel and paused to look in at the window. Something had caught her eye several days before and she had been debating whether to buy it. It was still in the window, a pale cream onyx box streaked with white and lined with dull red velvet, a perfect trinket-case for Marta. As she was looking at it the shop door opened and Karl came out. He smiled briefly and set off towards the hotel.

Karen bought the box and a silky scarf for Frau Leiter from further down the village and then very pleased with her purchases climbed the hill back to the Hotel Adler.

By evening the threatened snow was falling, drifting in swansdown flakes between the houses and sprinkling another layer of soft powder everywhere. Once again the pavements were smooth and white and trees bent under their extra load, but the guests were delighted for gentle snow floating down was exactly how they had imagined Christmas Eve in Austria. After dinner most of them donned their warmest clothes and boots and set off to the churchyard where the whole village gathered to sing carols in the snow. The bell was ringing to welcome them all, its chimes strangely muffled in the falling snow; no echoes reverberated from the surrounding mountains as the heavy clouds smothered the village like a thick blanket. The lights shone out from the windows of the church, shafts of coloured light patterned the snow and gleamed in the gold of the churchyard crosses, the black and gold wrought-iron crosses marking the village graves. Karen had left her guests to find their own way to the gathering; she felt such an evening was a very personal occasion and had no wish to make anyone feel that he or she ought to be there. She herself went across while the bell was still ringing and joined a group standing just inside the churchyard gates.

There was a low current of conversation as the crowd waited for the singing to start. Then it died away as music wafted on the air, very faint at first but growing louder as the town band processed round the square and through the narrow streets to the church perched on a rise guarding its village and villagers, living and dead. Behind the band came the village children, muffled in warm clothes against the snowy cold, but singing their hearts out. Behind the children straggled a long line of people, many of them carrying gifts to lay by the crib inside the church. Karen had explained to her guests that most Austrians gave their presents on Christmas Eve rather than Christmas Day and that many took a present to the church, and these were laid round the crib and distributed to hospitals and homes afterwards.

The singing was beautiful and, though many of the carols were unknown to the English in the crowd, some of the tunes were familiar and at the end the children sang 'Hark the Herald Angels sing' in English as a

Christmas gesture of goodwill to their English visitors. Immediately the singing swelled as everyone from England joined in and contributed his hymn for Christmas. When the singing was over the band continued to play softly as those who had brought gifts processed slowly into the church to lay them at the crib. Karen had heard someone near her in the crowd singing both in German and in English and turning now she found Karl at her elbow.

'It's a very beautiful service,' she said. 'The singing was lovely.'

He smiled. 'It's traditional,' he said simply. 'Come and see the crib,' and taking her arm he led her through the crowd to the church door. The last of those who had brought gifts were just coming out and the band was preparing to process back to the square. Karen followed Karl into the church. It was lit by hundreds of candles — on all the ledges and windowsills and in hanging candelabra, their flickering light making the ornate gilding of the church twinkle and flash. The crib was in one corner and now surrounded by the gifts which had been brought and laid out carefully on the floor. The tiny figures standing in the stable straw gazed serenely out at the offerings. Karen wished she had something to give, so calm and reassuring was that moment in the stillness of the church. Footsteps heralded the arrival of more people and the moment was gone. Without a word she and Karl turned from the crib and went back to the noise and bustle of the hotel.

10

Karl went through to the family's living-room and, after a quick glance into the lounge and the bar to assure herself that everyone was happy, Karen slipped upstairs to find the gifts she had bought for Marta and Frau Leiter. She had not decided exactly when she was going to give her presents, but she wanted to have them ready. As she came downstairs again Marta appeared in the hall and catching Karen's hand dragged her through to the family quarters.

'Come and see what Dad's given me,' she cried in excitement. 'It's so beautiful.' She pushed open the door into the living-room and still holding Karen's arm pulled her into the room.

'I've brought Karen in to see my present,' she cried to her father and grandmother who were seated by the fire. Karl stood up and Frau Leiter said, 'Karen, my dear, do come in. Happy Christmas to you.'

'Look, Karen,' said Marta, her eyes sparkling, and from a box on the table she lifted a tiny gold watch on a delicate chain.

'Isn't it the most beautiful thing in the world?' and she flung her arms round her father's neck and pressed her face against his cheek. His arms closed round her and for a moment Karen saw such tenderness in his eyes as he stroked his daughter's hair that she felt like an intruder on the family's Christmas and she turned away. Frau Leiter took her hand and led her to the fire.

'Here, Karen, we have something for you. Marta, where did you put Karen's present?' Marta bounced across the room, still bursting with excitement.

'Here on the mantelpiece,' and she reached down a small package. 'It's not much,' she said, handing it to Karen, 'but it comes with our love.' Karen unwrapped the parcel to find a tiny bottle of perfume, cut-glass with a little glass stopper.

'I hope you like it,' sang out Marta, still bubbling. 'If not we can change it.' Karen removed the stopper and, touching the perfume to her wrists, sniffed appreciatively. 'It's beautiful, Marta, thank you very much, and what a lovely bottle!' She smiled round at them and it was then she noticed Karl was no longer in the room.

'Daddy and I chose it together,' cried Marta. Karen felt a little uncomfortable as she had bought nothing for Karl, how was she to know . . . ? But she said cheerfully, 'Well thank you both. I have something for you too,' and delving into her capacious shoulder-bag she produced the two parcels she had wrapped so carefully that afternoon. Marta pounced on hers excitedly and, quickly stripping its paper, held the little onyx jewel-box in her hands.

'Oh, Karen, it's lovely,' the girl breathed and hugged her in delight.

'Look Oma, look what Karen's given me, I can keep my beautiful watch in it too. It couldn't be better. Oh thank you, Karen, thank you.'

Frau Leiter was pleased with her scarf and smiled at Karen. 'You needn't have bought me anything, my dear,' she said, 'but, as you have, I'm delighted. Thank you very much,' and she kissed Karen on the cheek. Feeling a little awkward Karen said that she had to go out to have a Christmas drink with her guests and Marta immediately said, 'I'll come too.' As they re-entered the hall Marta suddenly said, 'Karen, where's that twig you told me about?' Karen looked blank for a moment. 'What twig?'

'You know, the branch for kissing under.' Karen laughed.

'Oh, the mistletoe! I'd forgotten all about it. It's upstairs.'

'Do get it,' begged Marta. 'We can stick it up in the bar.' Karen looked dubious.

'Well,' she said, 'I don't know . . . '

'Go on,' urged Marta. 'It'll be fun — you can make everyone kiss each other.'

Karen allowed herself to be persuaded by Marta's enthusiasm, although with misgiving. What would Karl think of the idea? Well, she would soon find out. When she came down with the mistletoe she found Marta was already in the bar, practising her careful English on the two girls, Carolyn and Julie, who were awaiting the arrival of two Dutch boys they had met in ski-school. Karen was greeted with giggles from the three girls.

'Where shall we put it?'

'Somewhere central.'

'Somewhere accessible,' and they all laughed again.

'Over the door,' suggested Carolyn, 'and no one gets in without a kiss!'

'In the middle of the room,' laughed Julie, 'we might get more choice.'

Finally they decided that they would put it amongst the ivy round the light hanging in the middle of the ceiling and

Karen climbed up on a chair with a piece of string provided by Marta and suspended the twig amidst the ivy-leaves.

'What are you doing?' said a voice from the doorway so unexpectedly that all the girls jumped and started giggling again. It was Johann, and Marta had started explaining excitedly before she realised that he was not alone, that Hans-Peter had come with him to collect Charlotte and take her out.

'Sounds a splendid idea,' agreed Johann and catching Marta by the shoulders planted a kiss on both her cheeks. 'Yes,' he said consideringly, 'yes, it seems to work perfectly, but we'd better be sure,' and everybody laughed as with a gallant bow to each of the English girls he said, 'Ladies!' and proceeded to continue testing the mistletoe first with Carolyn and then with Julie. Hans-Peter stood awkwardly at the door, not wanting to become involved in the general hilarity and yet somehow unable to walk away. He kept his eyes well clear of Marta, afraid she would expect him to follow Johann's exuberant example. However, Marta maintained an energetic conversation with Karen, treating Hans-Peter to her back, until the bar began to fill up.

The two Dutch boys and the Drews came into the bar just then and Fritz the barman, who had been about to leave his post behind the bar to join in the fun, was kept busy whilst the newcomers, all laughing, made use of the mistletoe and wished each other Merry Christmas. Karen, perched on a stool by the bar, said, 'I'm surprised to see you, Johann. I thought you'd be busy tonight.' Johann shrugged his characteristic shrug. 'No point in keeping the bar open if there's nobody in it,' he said, 'far more fun to join you all over here. Not many local people go out on Christmas Eve, they're with their families, so Hans-Peter and I came across to join the tourists!' He laughed, a little bitterly, Karen thought, and went on, 'Hans-Peter's got a date with that Charlotte girl. I'd have thought he'd have seen enough of her on the slopes with their private lessons. Private lessons in what I might ask!' he added darkly, his blue eyes twinkling. 'Actually she's getting on rather well, she's got good natural balance and is quick to learn, when she's not being temperamental and throwing her ski-sticks about.'

'Does she do that?' asked Karen amused.

'When she can't do something first time, I understand,' said Johann.

'Will she manage the day out at Feldkirch?' asked Karen. 'I know she's determined to come.'

'Oh yes, I think so as long as we keep an eye on her. It's not a difficult run across the top, there are only one or two trouble spots and if she's helped over those she'll manage the rest all right. Actually it won't hurt her to discover she isn't as good as she thinks she is.' They were interrupted at that moment by the lady in question as Charlotte made another of her entrances, dressed in a very skimpy sleeveless frock and high-heeled sandals. When she saw what was going on she sauntered across to the mistletoe and standing beneath it beckoned to a very embarrassed Hans-Peter. 'Are you afraid to kiss me in public?' she demanded and when he complied with a peck on her cheek she cried indignantly, 'Not like that, like this,' and, pulling his head down to hers, slipped her arms round his neck and kissed him deeply and lingeringly on the lips. There was a stifled sob and Marta ran out of the room. Karen was about to follow her when Johann caught her hand and pulled her into the space just vacated by the triumphant Charlotte and her sheepish-looking Hans-Peter.

'You produced this marvellous branch, now it's your turn,' he said cheerfully and putting his arms round her he kissed Karen full on the mouth. It was not as sensuous a kiss as Charlotte had given Hans-Peter, but Karen was very much aware of a restrained strength within it. Johann tightened his arms around her fractionally before he released her and she felt the tension between them before he said lightly, 'Beware, my lovely, or I'll carry you off to my lair.'

'Your lair in the woods?' laughed Karen, but her laughter died away as she glanced up and caught a glimpse of Johann's face. She slipped free of his arms and sat back on a bar-stool and Johann laughed loudly and looking round the room he cried out, 'Who's next?'

'What are you all doing?' Karl's voice cut through the general laughter in the bar with undisguised amazement. Karen did not know how long he had been there, standing in the doorway, and wondered if he had seen her with Johann. She found she had a deep-rooted hope within her that he had not. The kiss had meant nothing, to her at least, and she did not want the severe-looking Karl Braun to think it had.

'Not the image he'd want for his hotel,' she tried to tell herself; but any further thoughts on the reason for her reluctance were cut short by Charlotte Armstrong who pounced on Karl with a cry of delight, 'Herr Braun is next?' and dragging him beneath the mistletoe she said by way of explanation, 'It's mistletoe, for kissing under,' and attempted to give the surprised Karl the same treatment she had meted out to Hans-Peter. However Karl, not unfamiliar with mistletoe, held her off and gravely planted a kiss on each of her cheeks and said, 'Merry Christmas, Miss Armstrong.' Taking courage from Charlotte Carolyn murmured to Julie, 'I think this one's a dish,' and she took Charlotte's place to receive Karl's Christmas wishes.

A moment later Karl joined Karen by the bar.

'Where's Marta?' he asked, perching on the stool next to hers. 'I thought she was here.' Karen's face hardened for a moment as she looked across the room to where Hans-Peter and Charlotte were ensconced in a corner, heads almost touching in the intimacy of their conversation. 'She was, in fact it was she who started the kissing game under the mistletoe, but it backfired on her because Charlotte came in to meet Hans-Peter and joined in rather too enthusiastically. She's proud of her conquest and lets no opportunity pass to parade it in front of Marta. Poor Marta was very upset.' Karl looked across at the slim young girl with her arms draped round Hans-Peter's shoulders, and repressed a comment with tightened lips. Karen saw he was angry but she did not make the mistake of offering to go after Marta this time. Left on her own she would have sought the girl out and tried to persuade her to brave the couple in the corner and come back into the bar to show how little the incident had meant, but, knowing how touchy Karl was about Marta, she decided to leave it to him and so she merely said, 'She probably went up to her room.' Karl nodded and then said, 'Why do they have to sit about here? You'd think Hans-Peter would take her out somewhere else.'

'I think he was going to,' replied Karen, 'but our Charlotte turned up wearing that dress and those ridiculous shoes, and she can't go far in those. You should have seen Hans-Peter's face as she came through the door.'

'Well, I'd better go and find Marta and see if I can cheer her up,' said Karl getting off the bar-stool. 'She mustn't let such a trivial incident spoil her Christmas.'

'It may not seem trivial to her,' ventured Karen, a little afraid that Karl might make matters worse.

'Don't worry,' said Karl, appearing to accept the implied warning, 'I'll go carefully.' He paused a moment and then said, 'I hope you have a very Happy Christmas here with us, Karen,' and before she realised what was happening they were under the mistle-toe. Karl rested his hands on her shoulders and kissed her lightly on her forehead and then briefly on the lips; then without another word he turned and went in search of Marta. Karen stood where she was for a moment, too stunned to move, watching his tall figure cross the room and disappear into the hall. In the general hubbub of the bar no one had seen Karl leave or noticed the way he had wished Karen 'Merry Christmas'. There was no diminution in the level of conversation, no curious glances across the room; in the most public of all the rooms their moment had been private yet to Karen it was the most shattering moment in her life. Suddenly she came face to face with the truth, a truth that she had perhaps already subconsciously rejected but now could no longer ignore. She loved Karl Braun. Loved him in a way she never had, never could have, loved Roger. She longed for the strength of his arms to keep her safe, she longed to soothe away the worried lines that so often creased his face, she longed to see him smile his special smile for her alone and the thought of being parted from him, living somewhere else, made her heart turn somersaults of anguish. There had been no pent-up emotion in his kisses as there had been in Johann's; his lips had been cool and gentle, for he was merely passing a seasonal greeting, but in the moment they touched her Karen knew she loved him and felt weak with the knowledge. Now glancing round the bar and seeing everyone involved in their own conversations she was thankful to slip away before anyone could speak to her and she climbed the stairs to the sanctuary of her bedroom to come to terms with the new situation.

11

Karen hardly slept at all that night. At first she sat gazing out of her unshuttered window at the snowflakes drifting aimlessly past, watching the layer of snow grow deeper on the sill. Then she went to bed and passed several more restless hours, her mind in a turmoil. Having acknowledged to herself her love for Karl, she had to consider what it would mean and came to several conclusions which she had to learn to accept.

That she loved him she had no doubt and the knowledge that he entertained no such feeling for her was also without doubt. His feeling of active dislike, she decided, had gone and the apprehension that she might not be up to her job had been misplaced, but he still loved and missed his first wife Anna and there had been nothing in his manner or behaviour to suggest that this would change. His kiss had been a Christmas greeting such as he had given the other girls only minutes before in the same bar, nothing more could be read into it, and this Karen knew and accepted, albeit with a heartache. Having established quite clearly in her mind the position of each of them in their relationship, such as it was, she went on to consider what she had to do next. One part of her cried out to escape, to run and hide, to try to forget him as she had tried and succeeded with Roger.

'Get out,' she told herself, 'before it's too late and you get hurt again.' But in her heart she knew it was already too late and, unless she built up strong defences and retreated behind them, being hurt was only a matter of time. Another more rational part of her said that she had to stay and keep her side of the bargain with Lambs International. She had promised Donald Keary she would stay until next winter and establish St Wilhelm as a prime resort, and there was no way in all conscience that she could back out of that now, particularly as Lambs had found her a job when she needed one. A third part of her whispered that at least she would be near Karl, see him every day, if she stuck to her original agreement. After all she was fairly certain he had no idea of the way she felt and provided that she kept him in ignorance there need be no embarrassment or awkwardness on either side.

By the time the grey dawn streaked the sky the snow had stopped and the clouds were gradually dispersing, pierced by the faint rays of an early sun, Karen had made her decision. She would stay, she would immerse herself in work and though this would bring her continually into contact with Karl she would treat him with cool reserve, preserving their friendship at a working level without allowing it to develop to a state which might reveal her heart to him. She had been rejected by one man and she was determined that no other should have the chance. Once her decision was made she drifted off into an uneasy sleep to awake tired, two hours later, to face Christmas Day.

In fact Christmas Day was little different from any other day. The lifts were running and there was ski-school for any who had survived the session in the bar the previous night. Karen spent the usual half hour or so in her kiosk after breakfast ready to answer any questions or deal with any complaints, but there was none, everyone was set for a peaceful day and looking forward to a 'Traditional English Christmas Dinner' in the evening. Marta wandered across and suggested Karen came into the kitchen for a cup of coffee. Karen hesitated, afraid that Karl might be there, but Marta pressed her, saying, 'Come on, Karen, you're not needed out here and anyway Dad's in the office if anyone wants anything.'

So Karen allowed herself to be persuaded and said, 'Just a quick one, and then I'm going skiing, I need the fresh air.' While they were drinking coffee and eating one of Frau Leiter's delicious pastries, Marta said, 'I'm sorry I got upset last night, it was just . . . ' and she stopped speaking as the tears welled up in her eyes once more. Dragging a damp handkerchief from her pocket she sobbed, 'I'm sorry, Karen, I can't help it, I hate her! Hate her! I hope she breaks her neck on the mountain,' and she blew her nose noisily. Karen took her hand. 'No you don't, you wouldn't wish that on anyone. Come on now, Marta, you were doing so well before. And remember she's not here for ever, she'll be gone soon.'

'And so will Hans-Peter,' cried Marta. Karen decided it was time to speak sharply.

'Now stop it, Marta. You must pull yourself together.' Shades of Marianne, thought Karen with a wry smile as she spoke.

After two more cups of coffee Marta was relatively cheerful again, looking forward to the fancy-dress party on New Year's Eve. She giggled, 'I could borrow Charlotte's ski-suit and go as a bitch!'

'Marta!' Her grandmother's voice cut through the air like a whipcrack. 'Don't let me hear you speak like that again. You shouldn't encourage her, Karen!' Karen, who had been startled to laughter by Marta's suggestion, said quickly, 'Don't worry, Frau Leiter, she was only joking. I'm going out now,' she went on smoothly, 'I'll see you later,' and, leaving Frau Leiter to deal with her granddaughter and her outrageous suggestions, escaped to the mountains, so uncompromising and majestic, to get her own tumbling thoughts into some sort of perspective.

She skied alone in spirit, unaware of others on the slopes, until the sun sank behind the peaks and the illusion of warmth it had maintained vanished in the creeping dusk. She took the last chair to the top and skied down towards the twinkling lights of the village, pausing occasionally to savour the peace of the now deserted hill. It was a clear night and traces of light which lingered in the sky were enough to throw the trees into sharp relief against the snow, but where she followed the track through the woods the darkness closed in eerily around her and, by the time she finally reached the village and shouldered her skis, night had fallen.

She reached the Adler to find Karl confronting Mrs Garfield in the main hall.

'No, I regret she is not here, Mrs Garfield. She is not on duty all twenty-four hours and today is Christmas Day. I'm sure you will not stop her a few hours off on such a day.' Karen stepped inside and Karl said with marked relief, 'Ah, here is Karen now,' and with no further explanation he retired to his office. Karen, as always, was impressed by Karl's slightly stilted yet fluent English. He always spoke English to the guests and they appreciated it, relieved not to have to try out their German.

Karen dealt with Mrs Garfield and then went upstairs to change for dinner. Her afternoon of freedom on the mountain, the hard physical exercise and the sharpness of the air had done their work well; Karen felt tired but at ease. She could face the next few days with a certain equanimity and after that as she gradually grew accustomed to her feelings she was sure she could settle into a pattern of life which would give her a sort of quiet happiness. She went down to join her guests for Christmas Dinner.

The next few days passed easily enough. There were the inevitable meetings with Karl to discuss the minor problems which arose daily, but most of these were routine and they were maintained at an almost impersonal level, polite, efficient and distant. Karen was glad to escape from each encounter without betraying her feelings though it did not get easier as she had hoped it might. She would catch herself studying Karl's serious face, waiting for his smile, and each time she had to turn her thoughts quickly to the subject on hand for fear he would notice her scrutiny. The meeting about the New Year's Eve fancy-dress party was held with the guests one evening in the bar. Karen explained the arrangements.

'We do want everyone to come in some sort of costume or the people who have bothered begin to feel silly.' There were groans of dismay along with the questions.

'Where do we get costumes from?'

'You haven't given us much warning!'

'What can we use to dress up?'

Karen laughed and said, 'Don't panic! No one is going to be able to come in a tailor-made outfit. This is part of the fun, isn't it?' she appealed to Karl. He nodded and Karen went on, 'We're not expecting Henry VIII or full-wigged cavaliers or anything like that. We're giving prizes for the best costume and the most ingenious one which are not necessarily the same thing.' There was a buzz of conversation and then Karl spoke in his accented English. 'You may borrow some things from the hotel. In the cupboard on the main landing is a basket of oddments we have collected over the years — a few hats and some pieces of material. You are welcome to help yourselves, but if you borrow something from anywhere else in the hotel we merely ask you to replace it the next day.'

'Give us some ideas,' said Carolyn, 'I don't know where to begin.'

'Well,' said Karen, 'I'll say nothing definite because it might spoil ideas people have already, but film characters, television, people from history, have all appeared before. If you can't think of anything, look in the basket Herr Braun mentioned and something there may give you inspiration.'

'Other people from the village will be here,' said Karl. 'The party is open to all. You change before or after dinner as you like and then the village will come.'

The gathering broke up into small groups, everyone discussing ideas, and several collected round Karen to question her about it. 'I wasn't here last year,' she insisted, 'so I don't know what to expect any more than you do, but I've been to others in other places and it couldn't matter less how makeshift your costume is. We don't want people spending hours and hours perfecting outfits, it's just a bit of fun.'

'Do you think they will all join in?' Karl's voice at her shoulder made Karen jump. He spoke in German now and she answered in the same language.

'I don't know, it takes quite a lot of encouragement sometimes to get the English to dress up, but I think we may have persuaded them to try. I've made a big poster for my board offering 'valuable prizes', so perhaps they'll be inspired.'

Karl laughed. 'What sort of valuable prizes?' he said.

'Oh I don't know yet, bottles of some sort, I expect.'

'Well, Rudi always gives a voucher to use in his shop so we can give that for something special. Are you busy now?' The change of subject was so abrupt that Karen almost said no, but she guessed, just before she spoke, that Karl had been going to suggest a drink together and, much as she would have loved to have him to herself for a little while, she would be breaking her resolution to keep their relationship on a strictly business basis. So she said, 'Well, I am a bit. I've got to go and see Johann about the outing to Feldkirch.'

'I thought that was all organised for the day after tomorrow.'

'Well it is almost, but I just wanted to run over the final details. It's my first trip outside the village, you know, and I want it all to go without a hitch.'

'I'm sure it will.' And Karl turned and went out of the bar without another word. Karen watched his retreating back and then gave herself a mental shake. If she was going to be able to stay on at the Hotel Adler there had to be no weakness in her attitude, she had to keep away from Karl as much as possible.

There was no sign of him in the entrance hall as she left for Johann's bar a few minutes later and there was no light under the office door when she crept back into the hotel later still. She felt a pang of loneliness as she remembered the quiet hour they had spent together in that office the night her guests arrived. She had wondered if he would be there again tonight. Part of her hoped he would not so that her resolution would remain firm, but the other half of her longed to find him working late as before, though she knew that if he asked her to join him her determination would fail. However, there was no sign of him and Karen went upstairs half relieved and half disappointed.

⋆ ⋆ ⋆

The day of the Feldkirch outing dawned bright and clear. A coach was coming to collect the skiers who were going and they were all gathered in the square carrying skis, sticks and packed lunches, looking forward to the day's skiing. It would be skiing with a difference, including some easy runs along tracks through the woods, some wide-open pistes across the mountain-side and one or two steep narrow stretches which would be navigated by the less experienced skiers with some trepidation. Johann had been round all the classes checking who wanted to go on the day's outing and he had suggested that neither of the beginners' classes should attempt the trip as parts of it would be too difficult. These two classes were staying in St Wilhelm and the two instructors who stayed with them were organising some races on the nursery slopes, with medals to be won. Charlotte had been determined to go on the Feldkirch outing and Johann passed her as competent thanks to the private lessons she had had with Hans-Peter. Now in the crisp mountain air she was the centre of a little group waiting for the bus to come. Her startling ski-suit gleamed in the morning sunlight and she seemed to draw people to her as if she were a magnet. Johann was with his instructors, discussing whether to split up the groups to ski back in their classes or merely to shepherd the whole group along making sure no one was left behind. For the moment Karen had nothing left to do and so she leaned on her skis, her face turned to the sun, soaking up its pale warmth. The coach arrived and there was a surge forward as skis were loaded on to the rack and everyone climbed inside. Just as the last few clambered aboard, Karen saw two figures approaching carrying skis. It was Karl and Marta. Karen caught her breath, she had not realised Karl was coming too. Perhaps he wasn't, merely seeing Marta off on the bus, but then her mind registered that they were both carrying skis. They climbed into the bus and the door clanged shut behind them.

'Is everybody here?' called out Johann in English. 'Answer me if you are not yet arrived.' There was a titter of laughter at this and Karen looking round the coach as it pulled slowly out of the little square felt as if she were back at school on one of the infrequent daytrips out. There was an air of barely suppressed high spirits with a great deal of laughter and loud voices.

The journey took half an hour by road because the coach had to descend the hairpin bends that led up to St Wilhelm from the valley below and then make a similar ascent up another winding road to the village of Feldkirch further round the mountain. Karen enjoyed the trip. The sky was a clear blue dome above them and the mountains and the valley were bathed in pale winter sunshine; a perfect day for skiing.

12

Feldkirch was a beautiful little village, smaller than St Wilhelm, but with the same wide-eaved houses crowding round the central square, their painted shutters thrown back seeking the winter sun. There were one or two bars with neon signs to attract the tourist eye, but otherwise the strange timeless quality of a small Tyrolean village prevailed. At one end of the main street past the few shops was a woodcarver's workshop, a noted local attraction which Johann pointed out as they passed, and at the other was an old onion-towered church beside which wound the road to the one chairlift that Feldkirch boasted. Johann had explained during the journey that the lift passes from St Wilhelm were valid in Feldkirch for this chairlift and the two drag-lifts further up the hill.

'There are several runs down from the top to the village,' said Johann, 'and they are all clearly marked both in direction and difficulty. We suggest you ski with friends for the rest of the morning and we will meet at the top cafe at lunchtime. You may eat your packed lunches there provided you buy a drink too. After lunch we make our classes again and ski back across the mountainside to St Wilhelm. Please do not be late — especially the lower classes. We do not want to start late because some people may take much time to ski all the way back.' As he was speaking Karen had time to admire his English. It was almost faultless if not always idiomatic; she wondered idly where he had learnt it.

Now he led the way to the chairlift followed by the skiers in twos and threes as they disentangled their skis from the heap the coach-driver had deposited on the pavement. Karen waited until she was sure that everyone had found skis and sticks before turning towards the lift herself. As she did she was hailed by Miss Emma Armstrong who had come with several other non-skiers to visit Feldkirch and then return to St Wilhelm on the coach.

'Please keep an eye on Charlotte for me, Karen.' She smiled a little ruefully. 'I know she's a bit of a nuisance, but the way she behaves isn't entirely her fault; still we won't go into that now. What worries me is the actual skiing; she hasn't done any before this year, do you really think she can manage this trek back to St Wilhelm?' Lines of worry creased Miss Emma's normally good-natured face and Karen felt a pang of sympathy for the poor woman in charge of so wilful and selfish a handful as Charlotte.

'Don't worry, Miss Armstrong,' Karen replied reassuringly. 'She'll manage all right. It's quite a long way but I understand that little of it presents much problem and we'll all be there to help her over any difficult parts. Those lessons she had with Hans-Peter have brought her on amazingly quickly and you can be sure Johann wouldn't have let her come unless he was satisfied she could cope.'

'Are you sure?' Miss Emma still looked a little doubtful. 'She can be very persuasive, you know.' Karen felt that dictatorial was more the word she would have used to describe Charlotte's method of getting her own way, but she did not say so, all she said was, 'Don't worry. The responsibility is ultimately Johann's and he wouldn't give in to her if he thought she couldn't manage, no matter what she said. Anyway, I'll keep an eye on her — she's not difficult to spot in that suit!' Miss Emma laughed.

'It is a bit bright,' she admitted. 'Thank you, Karen, then I'll leave her to you and enjoy my day here with a quiet mind.'

'That's all right, Miss Armstrong. And don't forget there's Hans-Peter too, he won't be far away from her, I don't expect.'

'Ah, that young man,' said Miss

Emma. 'She'll lead him a dance I expect. Well, my dear, I'll see you back at the hotel later. Enjoy your day.'

Miss Armstrong and her friends wandered off down the little main street towards the woodcarver's workshop and Karen shouldered her skis and set off up the hill towards the lift station. Most of the group were now swinging gently over the snowy trees up the hillside or were already safely at the top and it was only a few moments before Karen too was on her way up towards the dazzling slopes above. And dazzling they were as the sun was reflected from the snow with tingling brilliance and struck flashing fire from the icy patches where the loose powder snow had already been skied off. She could hear the crackle of ice under the skis of those skiers on their way down now and she knew that until the sun took the edge from the ice even the broad slopes would not be as easy as they appeared. At the top of the lift Karen glanced round for Charlotte and, keeping in mind her promise, when she saw her queuing to go up further on a T-bar drag-lift, she decided that perhaps she had better go up on the same lift and watch the girl until she was sure Charlotte could cope.

The T-bar was a doublesided drag-lift on a continuous moving cable. Skiers stepped forward in pairs and, placing the inverted T, which was on an extending cable, between them, were dragged firmly up the hill; without actually lifting them from the ground the T took their weight and the skis ran along smoothly uphill. Karen felt immediate misgivings when she saw that Charlotte had ended up paired with Marta. Although the two girls were much the same height and build, which would help when sharing a T-bar, Karen thought it might be a long ride up the hill for Marta, eaten with jealousy as she was for Charlotte, but she was too far away to intervene and as it turned out too far away to avert what happened next. The two girls moved forward to take the next T, which was handed to them by the liftman. Charlotte, unused to T-bars, had not lined her skis straight quickly enough and when the T jerked her forwards they were still crossed and she was tipped unceremoniously into the snow and, clutching at Marta as she fell, Charlotte managed to tip her off as well. Scarlet with rage and humiliation, Charlotte disentangled her skis, while Marta waited for her, and was finally ready to attempt the lift again. Karen wondered why, as several Ts had passed overhead before Charlotte was ready, Marta had not taken one of these and travelled up alone as so many people did if there was no one else there. She soon discovered. Marta, now in her worst school-girl mood was out to have her revenge on the miserable Charlotte. When they were both settled against the next T and had begun to move up the hill, Marta began her tricks. By shifting her weight from ski to ski with the ease and experience of a lifetime, she started to swing the T so that it twisted on its cable and jerked violently, catching Charlotte unawares and lifting her off the ground. Clutching the centre pole Charlotte managed to stay on her feet, but her skis got stuck in the tramlines of ice and she had no control over her feet; at a second jerk Charlotte was tipped sideways and travelled several yards with one ski in the air and the other sliding, uncontrolled, across the rutted ice. Many people would have fallen off, but Charlotte hung on with grim determination and, regaining her balance, kept her concentration absolute so that by the time they were reaching the top of the lift Marta had failed to dislodge her. However, just before they climbed the final mound to the level area where they would let go of the T and allow it to recoil to the overhead cable, Marta, without warning, slipped off and glided between the trees out on the open hillside. The sudden removal of her weight caused the T to twist again and Charlotte losing her battle found herself once more in the snow, being shouted at by the man on the T behind, to get off the track, and fast.

Karen was only two Ts behind, travelling up alone and so, when she reached Charlotte still floundering in the deep snow at the side of the lift-trail, she too slipped off and went to her aid. Charlotte was in a towering rage.

'How dare she! Little bitch! She did it on purpose!'

'I don't suppose she did, you know,' said Karen, who had watched Charlotte Armstrong meet her come uppance with some amusement. 'I expect she saw her father through the trees or something and forgetting you weren't used to these T-bars just slid off and skied through the wood to join him.'

Hans-Peter, who had gone up the lift ahead of Charlotte, was waiting impatiently at the top unaware of the incident which had happened just out of sight. Charlotte, still fuming, had to admit she had fallen off the T-bar twice and was further infuriated by his guffaw of laughter.

'Don't worry,' he said when he saw she was not in the least amused, 'all beginners fall off the drag-lifts the first time.'

'I didn't fall,' said Charlotte narrowly, 'I was tipped and I shan't forget it.' They set off down the hill and Karen followed behind to see how Charlotte got on. She was impressed, Charlotte had learnt fast and seemed to have natural balance; her turns were neat and confident and, though she hit one or two patches of ice which caused her to fall, she really coped very well. Her good temper seemed to be restored by her success, though Karen was well aware that the feud between the two girls, now openly declared, was not yet ended and that it no longer centred on Hans-Peter. He, the original cause, had been forgotten and only the battle remained.

Having decided Charlotte could ski

safely in the conditions, Karen skied both drag-lifts and the chair for the rest of the morning, delighting in her freedom and for an hour or so forgetting the nagging ache which her love for Karl had become. At lunchtime she found Marta sitting on the terrace of the mountain cafe at the top of the chairlift; her feet were stretched out in front of her, her sunglasses pushed up on to her hair and her eyes closed as she spread herself to the fleeting warmth of the midday sun. Karen dropped into a chair beside her and without preamble said, 'You're a naughty girl, Marta, you could have caused an accident.' Marta sat up with a jolt and said angrily, 'Don't talk to me like a child!'

'Then don't behave like one,' returned Karen. 'It took a long time to sort Charlotte out and get her to the top of that hill.'

'Good,' said Marta, unrepentant. 'Serves her right!'

'What does?' Karen had not heard

Karl approach and his voice made her jump. He put a glass of beer and another of fresh orange juice on to the table and pulled up a chair. 'What serves who right?'

Marta did not reply so Karen said, 'Marta tipped Charlotte off the T-bar this morning.'

'Won't hurt her,' remarked Karl. 'Do you want a drink, Karen?' Karen was growing used to his abrupt changes of conversation and so dismissing Charlotte from her mind she said, 'Yes, I'd love a fresh orange too, please.'

'Here, have this one,' and extracting some money from his pocket he gave it to Marta and said, 'Go and get yourself another, Marta, and something to eat too if you want it.'

It was a perfect day and, as she gazed round the cheerful groups of people hungrily eating their packed lunches and exchanging stories of the morning's skiing against a backdrop of slate-blue sky, smooth white snow and jagged mountain peaks, Karen felt that there was nowhere else on earth that she would rather be at that particular moment; with Karl at her side, and just now he was at her side, nothing could be improved upon. It was a perfect day.

At the next table Johann, Hans-Peter and Charlotte were together, Charlotte making a good deal of noise, with loud laughter and cries of delight as if she needed everyone to be aware of what a good time she was having; insecure or merely flaunting Hans-Peter in Marta's face, Karen wondered, she couldn't be sure, but she could see Marta was glowering at the group next to them and she wondered what mischief the girl was planning now.

As they were all preparing to leave for the trail back to St Wilhelm, Johann and Hans-Peter were seeing to their classes and for a moment or two Charlotte was left alone. She stood looking round, a little uncomfortably; she was not used to being left on her own even for a few moments and she did not like it. Karen was about to go and ask her how she had enjoyed her morning's skiing when she was forestalled by a tall man in a dark blue ski-suit. He was wearing sunglasses and had a hat pulled down over his ears, yet for some reason Karen felt that his face was familiar; for the moment, however, she was unable to place where she'd seen it before. Probably he was a German visitor staying at one of the guest-houses in the village and she'd seen him in the hotel bar. He spoke to Charlotte and Karen was near enough to hear him say in strongly accented English, 'You're too beautiful to stand alone. Come with me and we will drink.' 'Ah, the subtle approach,' thought Karen with a grin. But Charlotte did not mind about subtleties, she was still annoyed with Hans-Peter for laughing at her and so she said, 'How nice, I'd love a drink. A vodka, I think.' Karen blinked at her choice of drink, but the man did not bat an eyelid, he merely said, 'Of course. With tonic?' To which Charlotte replied bravely, 'Of course.'

'Let us go into this inn and have our drink. I will help you with the skis,' and placing a steadying hand on Charlotte's arm he bent down and released the skis which Hans-Peter had so recently put on for her. Karen was worried about this smooth pick-up and, remembering she had said she would keep an eye on Charlotte, she stepped forward and said, 'Charlotte, you really can't have another drink now, we're just off.' Charlotte's eyes flashed angrily at the remark and Karen wished she had worded it differently. 'You'll get left behind,' she said hastily, 'you can't keep everybody waiting.'

'I'll catch you up,' said Charlotte haughtily. 'It's not a difficult run, Hans-Peter said so.'

'Not with him there, perhaps,' said Karen, 'but you can't do it alone.' Before Charlotte could say more the man said, 'But I can show the young lady the way. I ski well. She will be safe with me.'

'You see,' said Charlotte triumphantly and started to walk back up to the terrace.

'Hey, Charlotte, where are you going?' Hans-Peter hissed across the snow on his skis. 'We're just going, come on.'

'I'm going in for a drink,' said Charlotte determinedly.

'This lady is with me,' announced the other man.

'Like hell she is,' snapped Hans-Peter. 'Charlotte, come here and put your skis on, the whole class is waiting.'

'No,' said Charlotte, but her voice faltered.

'Say that again,' said Hans-Peter, 'and you can add 'goodbye' to it.'

Charlotte flushed, but, weighing up his threat, decided to believe him. She turned her most devastating smile on the other man. 'Some other time perhaps,' she said in her best film-star manner. 'I'm at the Adler in St Wilhelm and I'm not always with him.'

The man forced a smile and said, 'I

quite understand, no doubt we shall drink together another time,' and he disappeared into the restaurant.

Charlotte put on her skis and sulkily joined her group and at last they set out. Karen was determined that Charlotte's silly behaviour should not spoil her perfect day and dismissed the irritating girl from her mind. She was safe with Hans-Peter, of that Karen had no doubt, which left her, Karen, free to join Karl and Marta for the run back to St Wilhelm. Karl had suggested it at lunchtime and under the spell of the perfect day Karen had agreed.

'We can ski across from here as the classes are doing,' said Karl, as they put on their skis a few moments later, 'or we can take the T-bar up to the top and come all the way down from there. It's a good run and joins up with the one from here further along.'

'Oh, let's take the route, Dad,' cried Marta. 'It's much better than from here and Karen would enjoy the gun-barrel.'

'What's the gun-barrel?' asked Karen

as she adjusted her sunglasses and pulled on her ski-gloves.

'Oh, it's a narrow gully round the other side of that outcrop of rock.' Karl pointed to a tongue of bare rock which jutted out near the top of the mountain and ran in a narrow spine along the ridge. 'If there aren't too many people it is a marvellous schuss, very steep but with a couple of outlets at the sides for safety. Classes take it very slowly, turning a lot and waiting from time to time for everyone to catch up. Obviously we can't schuss it if there are any classes, but if not it makes a most exciting run.' Karl was right. They stood at the top of the gun-barrel looking down. It was very narrow and dropped steeply. The sides rose like those of a ravine and along the top were a few stunted trees, twisted, clinging tipsily to the lip of the gully. Karen caught her breath as she looked down the long narrow trail. It was empty.

'Great!' breathed Marta, 'now we can fly!'

‘You go steady!’ warned Karl. ‘Karen and I don’t want to have to get the ‘blood wagon’ out to you.’ Marta laughed at the thought of being carried home on the ski-sledge used to transport injured skiers down the mountain. ‘Don’t worry, Dad. I’ll be careful.’

‘Well you go first, Karen can follow you and I’ll come last and pick up any pieces of either of you.’

Karen launched herself after Marta, who really did seem to be flying down the gun-barrel ahead of her; the walls of snow on either side flashed by as she gathered speed and crouching low over her skis she followed the red blur that was Marta. The gun-barrel was longer than it had appeared from the top and there was a steep curve to the right. Karen negotiated it easily enough and, by the time she screamed to a halt in a spray of snow beside Marta waiting at the end, she felt magnificent. The exhilaration of the speed made her feel quite lightheaded and she found she was laughing the unselfconscious laugh of a delighted girl, a laugh of pure joy. Marta turned to her with a look of surprise and said impulsively, 'Why, Karen, you're beautiful.' Karen was taken aback at her unexpected words, but before she could speak Karl had hissed past them without slowing, calling, 'Come on. Let's go,' and they sped after him across the smooth snow, and somewhere within her Karen wished the day would never end. At last Karl stopped at the edge of a ridge.

'There they are, all of them.' He pointed down the hill with his stick. Karen could see several groups further down negotiating a steep mogul-field and she wondered how Charlotte would cope with the strange hard snow humps which covered the steep slope just there. The three of them skied down to the last group which was Hans-Peter's. Charlotte was standing at the top of the mogul-field, staring down at it, wondering how on earth she was going to get down it to the safety of the trail through the woods at the bottom. Marta gave her a scornful look and calling, 'See you at the hotel,' swished her way neatly down through the moguls, turning with ease, apparently unaware of their existence. Karen saw Charlotte's face harden with determination as she saw Marta go. She overcame her fear and started unsteadily down the slope, encouraged at every turn by Hans-Peter. She fell several times but gradually gained a little confidence and turned awkwardly and slowly when he told her she arrived safely at the bottom. Karen had to admit that whatever else Charlotte lacked she had courage.

Karl and Karen took the trail through the woods at a leisurely pace, following Hans-Peter's group, which was moving much faster now as there were no difficult obstacles to negotiate; indeed some of the trail went uphill and they had to pull themselves along with their sticks. They skied in companionable silence and it was then Karen heard a noise over the hiss of their skis and she glanced up into the dark depths of the trees on the hill above them. She thought she saw a movement there but whoever or whatever it was remained hidden in the strange shadowy twilight and the usual utter stillness returned; perhaps she was imagining things. She glanced at Karl to see if he had noticed anything and catching her glance he smiled. She felt her heart turn over as she saw again how much younger he looked, how the creases changed to laughter-lines, how his expression softened and how, when he really smiled, his whole face was alight. Then she heard it again, the crack of a twig or branch up in the woods, and she looked up sharply but could see nothing.

'What's the matter?' asked Karl.

'It's silly I know,' she replied, 'but I think we're being followed.'

'Followed? By whom?'

'I don't know — I can't imagine, but I thought I saw someone just now, well a movement in the trees anyway, and

I've heard them several times, but I can't see anything or anyone. It's as if they were deliberately keeping hidden.' Karl stopped and Karen waited beside him. The last of Hans-Peter's group vanished round a corner and the forest silence descended. It was absolute.

'I think you must be imagining it,' said Karl after a minute. 'Probably a bird or something. Come on, this trail opens out on to the slopes above St Wilhelm. I'll race you back to the middle station.'

So they raced, shooting out from the dark shelter of the forest on to the wide open snow-field high above the village. The sudden expanse of snow was dazzling in the sunlight, but although Karen found herself blinking furiously for a moment neither she nor Karl slackened speed and they were soon overtaking the ski-school groups, who were preparing to descend at a more sedate pace. The sun had slipped behind the mountains and the air was sharp against Karen's face as she swooped down the hill, turning occasionally to avoid other skiers who were traversing, across her line of descent, but otherwise taking the shortest possible route. She could feel Karl at her heels and all her concentration was needed to keep ahead of him and she dared not look round. At last the piste narrowed to a trail leading to the chairlift middle station and, reaching the steps of the cafe, Karen swept to a standstill, to find Karl at her elbow laughing and crying, 'Dead-heat!' Karen agreed and they went up on the terrace in complete harmony to have a coffee before skiing the last slopes down to the village. The ski groups gradually arrived and at last the cafe was full of tired laughing people, but dusk was beginning to fall and, anxious to get his charges safely down to the village again, Johann hurried everyone until the terrace was left deserted and cold.

Karen and Karl arrived at the hotel together and were greeted by a distraught Miss Emma Armstrong in the foyer. One look at her face told Karen that her perfect day was over.

'Herr Braun, Karen, thank goodness you're back. Where's Charlotte?'

'Charlotte?' Karen looked surprised, she'd forgotten about Charlotte. 'She's with Hans-Peter, I think.' She looked at Karl for confirmation, and he nodded.

'Yes, Miss Armstrong.' He spoke in his careful English. 'We have seen her at the cafe at the middle station and she was with Hans-Peter.'

'What's the matter, Miss Armstrong?' asked Karen. 'Has something happened?'

'There's been a phone call from England. A very frightening phone call, I must find Charlotte at once, she may be in great danger.'

13

Karl took charge of the situation at once and suggested they all went into his office to hear exactly what had happened. Miss Armstrong allowed herself to be led into Karl's snug study and while he was settling her into one of the armchairs, Karen shut the door firmly behind them. Without asking, Karl went over to the corner table and poured Miss Armstrong a large brandy. She took the glass gratefully and after a few sips the colour began to seep back into her chalk-white cheeks.

'Now, please to tell us what has happened,' said Karl. 'Why is Charlotte in danger?'

'It's difficult to explain,' began Miss Armstrong. 'I hope you will understand.'

'I understand English very well if you do not speak fast,' replied Karl.

'I don't mean that exactly,' said Miss Armstrong. 'It's the whole situation.' She turned and addressed herself to Karen, who was perched on the edge of Karl's desk.

'I don't know if you know, but Charlotte's father is a top industrialist and she's his only child.'

'I did know, yes,' said Karen.

'Well, he's been having a good deal of trouble at one of his factories. There was a strike so he closed the plant and it was immediately described as a lock-out. You can imagine there was a lot of bad feeling about it.'

'Yes, I remember,' said Karen. 'I read about it in the papers just before I came out here. Is it still going on? I haven't ready any English papers since I arrived.'

'It is. There was almost a settlement sometime ago, but then the negotiations broke down for some reason.' Miss Armstrong paused for a moment and there was silence until Karl said, 'But what has this to do with Charlotte?'

'There's been a threat to kidnap her.'

‘Kidnap! What good would that do anybody?’ cried Karl.

‘Are they after money or what?’ asked Karen, equally puzzled.

‘Money? No not money,’ said Miss Armstrong wearily. ‘There’s far more to it than that, I’m sure. I don’t know what exactly, David wouldn’t say on the phone. All he did say was that he and Sandra, his wife, were coming out as soon as they could and that I was to keep Charlotte in the hotel and out of sight until they get here.’

A thoughtful silence filled the study for a few minutes and then Karl said, ‘If you do not mind, Miss Armstrong, I would like Frau Leiter, my mother-in-law, to hear of this news. It will be her responsibility too, you know.’

‘Of course,’ said Miss Armstrong, ‘but no one else.’

The situation was explained quickly to Frau Leiter with Karen acting as interpreter. Once she had got over her amazement, Frau Leiter became very practical.

‘First of all,’ she said briskly, ‘where is the child now?’

‘With Hans-Peter,’ said Karen. ‘I should think she’s safe enough with him, he won’t let her out of his sight, why only this afternoon . . . ’ Her voice trailed away as she realised what she had been going to say; then she turned to Karl and continuing to speak German she said, ‘I rather think they may be here already.’

‘Here? Who may be here?’

‘The kidnappers.’

‘What makes you say that?’ asked Karl sharply.

‘Well, a man tried to pick Charlotte up at the cafe in Feldkirch today.’

‘What? When?’

‘It may just be coincidence,’ said Karen. ‘He certainly wasn’t English, he spoke with an accent, so there’s probably no connection. I expect it was a genuine pick-up, if you see what I mean.’

‘The fact that he wasn’t English means nothing,’ said Karl. ‘They’d have to use someone with local knowledge. They could pay anyone.'

'What are you saying? What are you talking about?' asked Miss Armstrong, frustrated because she could not understand.

'Nothing much,' said Karen soothingly, not wanting to worry the woman more than she was already. 'We were discussing where Hans-Peter may have taken Charlotte. For a hot chocolate, I expect. She'll soon be back to change out of her ski-suit.'

'I suggest you go and see if you can find her, Karen, if that will set Miss Armstrong's mind at rest,' said Frau Leiter. 'It is best that she is here and remains here in the hotel until her parents arrive. I will serve her meals in her bedroom if you are really worried for her safety and don't want her to be seen in the dining-room.' Karen translated for Miss Armstrong and added, 'I'll go and look for her now and bring her back with me. In the meantime perhaps you'd like to go up to your room and wait there and Frau Leiter will send up some tea or hot chocolate.'

'You may have difficulty persuading her to come back with you,' said Miss Armstrong, 'and I don't intend to tell her the whole truth anyway, so perhaps you'd better tell her I'm ill and need her; that way she can't refuse to come and no one will think it strange that she's been asked to.'

'All right,' agreed Karen, 'that's what I'll say,' and, leaving Miss Armstrong to Karl and Frau Leiter, she set off round the village in search of Charlotte.

It was bitterly cold now and Karen was tired after her day's skiing. She hoped Charlotte would be easy to find so that she could get back and soak in the hot bath she had promised herself. The village square was very busy in spite of the cold. The lighted shops were open and doing brisk trade as all the skiers were tempted on their way home. As Karen passed the delicatessen the strange, indefinable smell of spiced meats and pickled vegetables wafted out on the night air and had she not been on a definite errand she would have succumbed to temptation and bought one of the toasted ham and cheese sandwiches being served at the counter. Several times she thought she saw Charlotte in a group ambling along the pavement, but the ski-suits that caught her eye were merely white, not the dazzling silver and gold of Charlotte's. She looked in through the windows of Rudi's to see if the girl was spending more money on equipment, but there was no sign of her.

'She's probably at Johann's,' thought Karen and branched off down the alleyway to Johann's bar. She pushed the door, but it was still locked and then she realised that there were no lights gleaming from behind the wooden shutters. Johann's bar was closed, presumably because Johann was not home yet.

'That's odd,' thought Karen. 'There's an old woman from further down the village who looks after the place while

Johann is with the ski-school.' She rattled the door once again to be sure there was no one there and then turned away disappointed; Hans-Peter and Charlotte were certainly not there, which meant she would have to try all the bars and cafes in the village to find them. She felt a nagging worry growing at the back of her mind, supposing Charlotte was not with Hans-Peter. Supposing she and Hans-Peter had had a row over his ultimatum on the hill at Feldkirch and she had walked out. Supposing the strange man on the hill had found her again. Karen felt a sudden wave of panic rising within her. Supposing the kidnappers had already got Charlotte. Karen was not sure how seriously she took the threatened kidnap, but this last thought made her quicken her step so that she was almost running from place to place, peering anxiously across crowded rooms filled with smoke and talk and laughter.

At last she found them. Charlotte and Hans-Peter, still together, came walking up a little side-street into the main square and Karen saw them as she emerged from the Drop Inn Disco. She hurried across to them and her call made them turn.

'Charlotte! Hey, Charlotte, wait a minute.' They waited for Karen to catch up and panting a little she explained that Charlotte's aunt was ill and needed her niece back at the hotel.

'What's the matter with her?' demanded Charlotte.

'I'm not sure,' answered Karen truthfully, 'but she didn't look very well when I saw her just now and she asked me to come out to find you.'

'What can I do?' asked Charlotte irritably.

'Come back and see her.' Karen had difficulty in keeping the anger out of her voice, but she was certain if she allowed it to show Charlotte would walk away again and might not come back for hours. 'She wants to see you; you know how a familiar face helps if you don't feel well in a strange place.'

'Of course you must go,' said Hans-Peter, 'you were going back to change anyway. I'll be over later to fetch you and perhaps we'll go bowling, there's a bowling-alley at Rheindorf — we'll go in my car.'

Charlotte laughed. 'In that clapped-out old thing?'

'It'll get us there,' said Hans-Peter, 'don't you worry. Wear something you can bowl in,' he added, remembering the unsuitable clothes in which she had appeared on Christmas Eve.

'All right,' said Charlotte grudgingly. 'See you later.'

'See you later,' said Hans-Peter. 'I hope your aunt will soon recover.'

Karen hustled Charlotte back to the hotel. She would leave it to Miss Emma Armstrong to break it to her niece that there would be no bowling tonight, nor skiing tomorrow, not a task Karen would have relished. There was no one in the foyer as they entered the hotel and the office door was closed. Charlotte went up to her aunt's room and Karen was about to tap on Karl's door when Frau Leiter came through from the kitchen.

'Did you find her?' she demanded.

'Yes, I found her. Luckily she was still with Hans-Peter. He's coming over to collect her later to go bowling, but I left the aunt to tell her she can't go.'

'Very wise,' nodded Frau Leiter. 'After all it's got nothing to do with us. Do you think that child's in danger?'

Karen shrugged. 'I don't know. It all sounds a bit dramatic to me, but I suppose these things do happen. Miss Armstrong certainly believes she is and she'll keep Charlotte here in the hotel until her parents arrive.'

'I can't say I blame her,' said Frau Leiter. 'It's only for a day and she is Miss Armstrong's responsibility after all. I would if she were mine.' Frau Leiter turned towards the bar. 'I'll tell Karl you've found her and she's safely in the hotel.'

'Thank you,' said Karen and went upstairs to her long-awaited bath, to soak away the tiredness from her body and to relax her mind in the soothing warmth.

As Karen had predicted, Charlotte did not take kindly to being restricted to the hotel. Miss Armstrong had not mentioned the threat of kidnap, mistakenly, Karen thought privately, because her brother Sir David, had told her not to frighten the child. She merely told Charlotte that she felt most unwell and that she'd be grateful if she, Charlotte, would sit with her for the evening.

'I'm going out,' said Charlotte stubbornly.

'I'd rather you didn't, dear,' said Miss Armstrong. 'It's only for one evening and I have another surprise for you.'

'What's that?' demanded Charlotte rudely.

'Well, your father and mother telephoned this evening, dear, and they've managed to get away for a few days after all. They're coming to spend New Year with us, isn't that splendid?' Charlotte greeted the news with mixed feelings. She was fond of her parents and often wished they did more things as a family, but they did restrict her freedom, because for all her loud boasting that she was allowed to do as she liked she knew that when her father was with her it was definitely not the case; he kept her on a much tighter rein than she liked to admit even to herself. On the other hand she longed to show off her new skis and what she could do on them, for her progress in that direction had pleased her and given her great satisfaction, even though with unusual humility she recognised that she had a long way to go. 'They don't know what time they'll be arriving so they've suggested we stay in the hotel until they get here.'

'You mean not go skiing tomorrow?' Charlotte was aghast. 'But I don't want to miss a day. I'll see them when I get back.'

'I'm sorry, my dear,' Aunt Emma spoke quite firmly, 'your father particularly asked that you should stay in the hotel until he gets here.' Even though at a distance her father was not as formidable as he could be close to, Charlotte felt the force of the request and recognised it as an order.

'Never mind, they may be here quite early and you can take them skiing with you. Your father used to be quite good; I don't know about your mother. And in the meantime you can make yourself a really good costume for the fancy-dress party tomorrow. Have you any ideas? I thought I'd go as Florence Nightingale, it would be easy enough.' She rambled on trying to excite her niece's interest, but Charlotte's mind was running on an entirely different track. Suppose Hans-Peter came tonight and found her unable to go bowling; he might take that weepy little fool Marta instead. The idea was too awful to be contemplated. Breaking into her aunt's monologue, Charlotte said, 'I'm going to change, Aunt Emma, and have a bath. It's been a tiring day. I'll come and see you again later.'

Realising that she might just manage to keep Charlotte within the confines of the hotel, but never in her room, Miss Emma decided she could not be ill any longer and, saying she felt better after the tea Frau Leiter had sent up to her, she emerged from her bedroom to join Charlotte in the dining-room and to pick at the dinner set before her. Karen, watching from her table tucked away in the corner, could sense the constraint between the two. Charlotte looked sulky, she was wearing warm trousers, a skinny poloneck sweater and some flat shoes, and Karen felt she was dressed to go bowling in spite of her aunt. Miss Emma Armstrong looked calm yet determined, as if she too had recognised Charlotte's intentions and was set to do battle against them. After the meal they took coffee by the smouldering log fire in the lounge. There was a murmur of conversation round the room, but the Armstrongs sat in silence with Charlotte glancing up expectantly every time the front door opened. At last Hans-Peter arrived and Charlotte, jumping to her feet, hurried out into the hall to meet him. Her aunt rose and walked out slowly behind her. Charlotte was explaining what had happened in an excited babble when her aunt interrupted smoothly. 'Good-evening, Hans-Peter.'

'Good-evening, Miss Armstrong.'

Charlotte ignored the interruption and continued her torrent of words; but her aunt's voice cut across the flow so sharply that Charlotte stopped speaking mid-sentence, astonished for a moment into thinking it was her father who addressed her.

'Charlotte! Be quiet! I'm speaking.' Miss Armstrong turned again to Hans-Peter. 'I'm so sorry, Hans-Peter, Charlotte is unable to go out this evening. I have not been well and would prefer she remain in the hotel so that I can call on her if I need her.' Aunt Emma, looking anything but unwell, then added, speaking to Charlotte, 'I'll sit quietly in the lounge, while you and Hans-Peter enjoy yourselves in the bar or down in the keller-bar.'

Karen had to admire the way Miss Armstrong had handled the situation and came to realise that there must be more of her brother in her than immediately met the eye. Hans-Peter led the rebellious Charlotte into the bar, Miss Armstrong went back into the lounge to finish her coffee and the whole evening was resolved.

14

The next morning brought another perfect skiing day and Karen, seeing Charlotte reading in the hotel lounge, was sorry for the girl, confined as she was to the hotel all day. The bright sunshine and crisp air were enticing and Karen was glad she had errands which would take her into the village even though she had no chance of skiing that day. She had to buy some prizes for the fancy-dress party that evening and being out in the open she felt released from the strange drama going on in the hotel. She wished she had not been told of the kidnap threat, for although it was not really her problem she felt involved, as she carried a certain responsibility for her guests' well-being. She considered contacting Lambs in London about the situation; but what could she say? There was no definite evidence and until Sir David arrived there would be nothing more; and by then it would be his responsibility anyway. There was nothing Lambs could do, nor Karen herself for that matter, though there was a nagging at the back of her mind; she was sure she had recognised the man who had spoken to Charlotte at Feldkirch though she could not for the life of her place where she had seen him before. She decided to tell Karl next time she saw him and in the meantime she set out to choose some interesting prizes for the costumes and the games at the New Year's Eve party. When she returned to the hotel with her prizes, Karen saw Charlotte and Hans-Peter chatting together in the hall; apparently Hans-Peter had dropped in after the morning's skiing to share a drink with the house-bound Charlotte, for as Karen crossed the hall to the stairs they moved into the bar. Karen could not help being sorry for the girl, confined to the hotel with little more than a transparent excuse for a reason. She wondered that such a headstrong girl as Charlotte seemed to be had not defied her aunt's instructions and gone out anyway. Short of actually locking her into her bedroom there would be no way of keeping her indoors and, as there were two other exits from the hotel quite apart from the front doors on to the square, she would have little difficulty in slipping away unnoticed. However, she seemed to have accepted, if ungraciously, the dictates of her aunt and appeared in the dining-room at lunchtime looking less resentful and more her usual self.

'I've thought of a marvellous idea for a costume, Aunt Emma,' she announced clearly enough to acquaint the whole dining-room with the fact. 'And I'm going to spend the afternoon making it, in my room. You're not to come in and peep,' she added firmly. 'I shan't let you see it until it's finished, then I'll come in to you for a dress parade.' Her aunt approved the idea with relief, glad to see Charlotte's natural good spirits return. 'I'm going to win that prize tonight,' Charlotte went on and then turning in her chair she called across to Karen, seated at her little corner-table. 'What's the prize for the best woman's costume tonight, Karen?' Her voice carried clearly and a momentary hush fell as everyone waited to hear the reply. But Karen would not be drawn. 'Wait and see,' she said with a smile and continued to eat her lunch. General conversation broke out again, but after lunch Miss Emma Armstrong beckoned Karen over to her table. Charlotte had vanished and Miss Emma invited Karen to join her for a cup of coffee.

'I've had another call,' she said in a low voice. 'David'll be here this evening at about dinner-time or soon after he hopes.'

'Oh good,' said Karen, knowing it would be a relief for all of them when Sir David Armstrong arrived and Charlotte's safety ceased to be their responsibility.

'Charlotte'll be busy this afternoon anyway,' said Miss Emma. 'She's going tonight as someone called 'Wonder Woman', does that mean anything to you?'

Karen laughed. 'Oh yes, it'll suit her very well,' and she smiled as she visualised Charlotte clad in boots and a bikini taking the entire village by storm, 'she's almost certain to win.'

'Thank goodness for that,' sighed Miss Armstrong. 'It'll completely restore her good humour if she's the centre of attraction tonight. Then there's nothing more to be done until David and Sandra arrive.' And with this false sense of security she sat back to enjoy a second cup of coffee.

Leaving Miss Armstrong seated comfortably over her coffee, Karen went upstairs to try on her own New Year's Eve costume. It was all a fraud really because she had nothing to do with choosing or making it. Each woman rep for Lambs International was given a 'shepherdess' costume to wear at the fancy-dress parties arranged in the various resorts. 'Little Bo Peep' looking after her 'Lambs' always got a laugh and was appreciated by the guests. Karen slipped into her costume and studied herself in the mirror. She would do, though she always felt stupid in the calf-length skirt with the pantalettes peeping below. She wondered what Karl would think of it and gave herself a mental rap over the knuckles for even allowing herself to consider his reaction; it was the sort of indulgence she could not afford if she was going to remain in his hotel. She changed back into her slacks and sat down to some of her more pressing paperwork.

Marta was bored. She had her costume for the evening already prepared. Having had the advantage of knowing there was always a New Year's Eve party, her Turkish slave outfit was laid out on her bed and she had nothing to do until the evening. She wandered around the almost deserted hotel and at length decided it was too nice an afternoon to stay indoors so she sought out Karen to go skiing, but Karen was too busy and promised to ski with her tomorrow.

'I really must do this paperwork, Marta. I've new guests coming in a couple of days.'

'All right,' said Marta with a sigh and she left Karen to it.

By the time she had caught up with her work Karen decided, as it was definitely too late to ski, she would have half-an-hour's sleep before putting in her early evening appearance in the kiosk to answer questions. She was tired and slept far longer than she had intended and when she awoke it was to find the room in dusky shadow with the lights in the square gleaming through her uncurtained window. Someone was knocking loudly on her door and calling her name. Karen recognised Frau Leiter's voice and flicking on her bedside lamp she quickly opened the door.

'Oh thank goodness you're here,'

cried Frau Leiter. 'Miss Armstrong is in the office with Karl. You must come at once. Charlotte is missing.'

'What!' exclaimed Karen. 'Oh no! I'll be down at once.' She dragged a comb through her sleep-tousled hair and followed Frau Leiter downstairs.

In the office she was greeted by Karl looking very grave and Miss Emma Armstrong distraught.

'Have you seen her, Karen?' cried Miss Armstrong. 'Have you seen Charlotte? Has she been with you this afternoon?'

Karen spoke gently. 'No, I'm afraid not, Miss Armstrong. I've been in my room all afternoon. When did you last see her? Are you sure she's not in the hotel somewhere seeing to her costume.' She turned to Karl and asked hopelessly, 'Have you searched?'

He nodded. 'Of course, unless she is deliberately hiding she is not in the hotel.'

'Might she have gone skiing, in spite of what you said?' Karen asked Miss

Armstrong. 'Once she knew you were safely in your room she could easily have slipped out. It was a beautiful afternoon, she could well have been tempted.'

'But it's dark outside now,' wailed Miss Armstrong, 'she'd have been back to change by now.' Karen snapped her fingers.

'Of course,' she said, 'has her ski-suit gone?'

'I — I don't think . . . I don't know, I didn't look, it never crossed my mind. When she wasn't in her room I suppose I panicked, and came to see if she was down here.'

'I'll go and look,' said Karen soothingly. 'Now try to be calm — she's probably gone skiing and then stopped for a hot chocolate with Hans-Peter on the way home, like she did yesterday.' She left Miss Armstrong to the ministrations of Frau Leiter and went upstairs to Charlotte's room. A quick glance told her that the ski-suit was not there, but she searched through the overflowing wardrobe to be absolutely certain; nor was the suit among the heaps of clothes strewn carelessly across the chairs and bed.

'Little madam,' thought Karen. 'She obviously went skiing, meaning to be home before she was missed.' She went back down to the office and was met by Karl in the hall.

'Has the suit gone?' he asked in a low voice.

'Yes,' answered Karen, 'she must have . . . '

'But her boots and skis have not.'

'What?' cried Karen.

'Sssh.' Karl took her arm and led her away from the office door. She felt a tingle run through her at his touch but Karl noticed nothing and went on, 'Her boots and skis are still in the ski-room.'

'Then she must be about the village somewhere. She can't be far.' Karen spoke with more certainty than she felt. 'We'd better go and look.'

'What about Miss Armstrong? How much do we tell her?'

'Let's just say that she's wearing the suit so she must be in the village and we're going to find her. There's no need to mention that she can't have gone skiing yet, is there?'

'All right, I'll tell her,' said Karl, turning back towards the office.

'Oh Karl . . . ' It was the first time she had called him Karl although she always thought of him by his given name, but in the stress of the moment she did not realise she had now actually said it aloud and he gave no sign that he had noticed the change, he merely glanced enquiringly over his shoulder.

'I don't know if it's important or not, probably not, but I thought I recognised the man who tried to pick Charlotte up at the Feldkirch cafe.'

'Why didn't you say so before?' said Karl in surprise. 'Who was he?'

'Well,' said Karen, 'that's the thing, I don't know, at least I'm sure I've seen his face before, but I can't place where. I may be entirely wrong and he simply bears a likeness to somebody . . . ' She shrugged.

'But you don't think so?'

'No.'

'Well,' said Karl consideringly, 'keep trying to remember where you've seen him before, it may be a slight lead, but until you do I see no point in adding to Miss Armstrong's worries, do you?'

They scoured the village, dividing the cafes and bars between them, looking into the shops and asking anyone they met from the hotel if he or she had seen Charlotte or Hans-Peter. The village had an air of excited expectancy as everyone bustled about preparing for New Year's Eve celebrations. It was a bitterly cold night with clear sky and an enormous moon creeping over the horizon, turning the snow on the mountain slope to a dull yellow. Gradually the streets emptied as people sought the warmth of their fires and a good meal to set them up for the later festivities. Karen was just on her way back across the square when she bumped into Johann. His bar had been on Karl's list, but she asked him anyway if Hans-Peter had come home from skiing yet.

'As far as I know he didn't ski this afternoon,' replied Johann. 'He said he was driving down to the valley for some reason or other. What's the problem? Why are you all looking for him and that little girl? Karl's just been in asking.'

'We're not looking for him only for her,' said Karen. 'Her aunt's ill and is worried that she's not back from skiing yet.'

Johann grinned. 'No doubt dazzling some poor man into buying her a drink somewhere. Have you seen the way she uses her eyes?'

'I've seen,' said Karen drily. 'Well, I must get back and see if Karl's found her,' and she hurried back to the hotel.

They gathered again in Karl's office but no one had any more news of the missing girl. They were just discussing what to do next when Karl suddenly leapt to his feet and darted out into the hall crying, 'Here she is!' They all rushed out after him and confronted Charlotte stealing across the hall towards the stairs. She looked round at the angry faces blazing at her and stood speechless with surprise. The silence was broken by Aunt Emma who spoke very softly and distinctly. 'Where the hell have you been?' It was some measure of her anxiety that she used such language, and to her niece. Miss Emma Armstrong was no weakling, but strong language did not come from her naturally. Charlotte, amazed by the unexpected strength of the query, tried to assume an innocent air and said, 'I went shopping — in the valley with Hans-Peter.' She glanced over her shoulder to the front door where Hans-Peter was standing dumbfounded at this reception committee. Her voice was tinged with defiance and her aunt, now entirely in control of herself again, once she was assured of her niece's safety, said, in the same dangerously low voice she had used before, 'Go to your room. Wait for me there.' For a moment Karen thought that Charlotte was going to stand her ground, but her nerve broke and she fled upstairs, away from the angry, accusing eyes staring across the hall. Miss Emma Armstrong was still apologising to Karen, Karl and Frau Leiter when Charlotte suddenly reappeared on the stairs, all defiance replaced by anger.

'It's gone,' she cried in fury. 'Search the hotel, somebody's stolen my ski-suit.' It was then that they all realised Charlotte was not dressed in the silver suit as they had supposed.

'What!' Karen spoke sharply as the glimmer of a terrible thought flickered at the back of her mind. 'What did you say?'

'I said,' Charlotte spoke clearly, enunciating her words as if she were addressing a backward child, 'somebody has stolen my ski-suit, and,' she added as an afterthought, 'I bet it was that stupid little Marta.'

Her words reminded Karen of the visit from Marta after lunch and that Charlotte's boots and skis were still in the ski-room, and the dreadful possibility became an overpowering certainty as it grew in her mind. She turned to Frau Leiter and Karl who were still standing together by the office door.

'Where is Marta?' she said simply. 'Has anyone seen Marta?'

15

It took a while for the implication of Karen's question to make any impression on Karl and his mother-in-law and as she was speaking in German Charlotte and her aunt had no idea of what she was saying. Charlotte continued to rail against the presumed thief, Marta, but Miss Emma saw at once that something was wrong even though she did not understand what, and she turned sharply to Charlotte. 'Be quiet, Charlotte. You've caused enough trouble for one day. If you'd been in your room, nobody could have taken your precious ski-suit. Go up now and I'll join you in a moment or two.' Charlotte scowled and continued to mutter under her breath but she obeyed her aunt and climbed the stairs once more.

'What has happened?' demanded

Miss Armstrong, turning her attention to Karen again.

'Nothing, that we know of,' said Karen, trying to sound reassuring, but her voice carried no conviction. 'It's just that Herr Braun's daughter went skiing this afternoon and hasn't come home yet. She's probably having a hot chocolate with a friend or something. Nothing to worry about.' But the expression on Karl's face belied her words and Miss Armstrong was not slow to make the same deductions as Karen. 'You mean the silly girl borrowed Charlotte's suit and you're afraid for her safety.' Karen shook her head.

'Really, I expect she's with a friend, though I'm afraid I do think she may have borrowed the suit; as sort of petty revenge on Charlotte for taking Hans-Peter.' Speaking of Hans-Peter reminded Karen he had been there earlier, and she looked round for him but he had beaten a strategic retreat and there was no sign of him.

'The suit couldn't matter less as long

as the child is safe,' said Miss Armstrong. 'I'll go up and deal with Charlotte. Despite what her father said, I think it is time she was told and she can see what her irresponsible behaviour has led to.'

Karl and Frau Leiter had retired to the office and Karen followed them there unbidden; they accepted her presence as entirely natural. She was involved and they needed her. The worried lines creasing Karl's good-looking face, so strongly defined, so deeply carved, made Karen's heart lurch. She longed to put her arms round him and soothe away his fears, like those of a frightened child. She could see the faintly haunted look in his eyes as if he were reproaching himself for Marta's disappearance. Karen ached for his pain and wished desperately there was something she could do or say to alleviate it. It was absolutely clear to her now how much Marta meant to him, the only part of Anna left to him and he was perhaps in danger of losing her too. Karen felt at a complete loss, knowing it was not for her to comfort him, particularly in the circumstances, yet aching to do so.

'Perhaps she's somewhere in the village,' she said lamely and then wished she hadn't spoken for her words broke the brittle silence like machine-gun fire. However Frau Leiter tried to fan the spark of hope. 'Perhaps she did not even take the suit.'

Karl drew a deep breath and seemed to fight for a few seconds to make his voice sound normal before he spoke.

'She's not in the village, that, I think, we must accept. We'd have seen her ourselves when we were searching for Charlotte. After all it was the suit that we were looking for really, rather than the person inside it.'

'She could be at someone's house,' suggested Frau Leiter.

'She could,' agreed Karl, 'but it's unlikely on New Year's Eve, with everyone getting ready to celebrate, here or somewhere else.'

‘We can search again,’ said Karen, ‘this time looking for Marta rather than Charlotte or the ski-suit. After all Frau Leiter’s right, we don’t know for certain that she’s got it on.’

A burst of laughter from the hall made them turn and glance out of the office door and brought them back to the realities of the evening; in the hall were several of the guests already dressed up in peculiar and ingenious disguises, for although the fancy-dress part of the evening did not start until after dinner, some of them had decided to eat wearing their costumes. Karl had a hotel to run, a hotel where there was to be a party, one of the most important of the season involving both guests and people from the village. Karen decided to risk a rebuke and spoke softly but determinedly to Karl.

‘You can’t go looking for her now; your place is here, but we must know she’s safe, so I’ll go. I’m not needed until after dinner. Let me go round again and you can tell me where her particular friends live.' She held up her hand as Karl tried to protest. 'I'll find her.'

'It makes sense, Karl,' said Frau Leiter gently. 'We do need you here. Let Karen go — for now anyway.' Her final words robbed her earlier ones of any comfort that they might have held, but Karl accepted their arguments. His grim face softened a little and he said quietly, 'Thank you, Karen.'

Armed with a list of her friends' addresses, Karen set out to search the village for Marta. The moon was higher now, sailing clear of the mountain crests and gleaming silver instead of with its earlier golden glow. The village seemed deserted as Karen hurried from house to house, from bar to bar, with only the soft creak of the snow under her boots for company. Everywhere she went she met with the same reply, no one had seen Marta, until at last she happened to meet Heinrich, the man who worked the chairlift, in one of the bars. 'Marta Braun? Yes, I saw her early this afternoon. She went up to the top station I think; wearing some flashy ski-suit, she were, like that English bit up at the hotel. All suns and moons and that.'

'Are you sure?' cried Karen, delighted at last to have some news, good or bad.

''Course I'm sure, known the child all her life, haven't I? I said to 'er 'that's a flashy suit, Marta' and she just grinned — not a word, just a grin and a wink. I reckon,' said Heinrich taking a long pull at his beer, 'I reckon that she borrowed that suit. Not really her line, she looked quite good in it.'

Karen thanked him and rushed back to the Hotel Adler. Karl was in the bar surrounded by a very cheerful group of his guests, all of whom were encouraging the spirit of the evening with spirit of another sort. As soon as he saw Karen he excused himself from the group and led her quickly to the office.

'Any news?' He crossed to his corner-table and splashed brandy into two glasses. As he handed one to Karen he touched her hand and said, 'You poor girl, you're frozen,' and, taking the glass back from her, he chafed her hands between his, while Karen answered his question. 'Some, and not very good. Heinrich at the chairlift saw her, wearing Charlotte's suit, but that was early this afternoon. As far as I can discover, no one has seen her since.' She spoke softly and her voice trailed away to nothing. Karl handed her back her brandy and picked up his own. A silence descended, filling the room to suffocation-point as neither was willing to put the fears of both into words. The shouts of laughter came clearly from the bar, and then louder still as a group of merrymakers crossed to the dining-room for dinner.

'Perhaps she fell,' said Karen suddenly. 'perhaps she had an accident.'

'Someone would have seen her, or heard her,' said Karl irritably. 'The hill was crawling with people this afternoon.'

'I know it's unlikely,' agreed Karen,

'but it is a possibility. Shouldn't we organise a search-party in case? I mean it's bitterly cold tonight and if she were lying hurt somewhere . . . '

'Well,' said Karl, 'perhaps — though they won't be able to do much in the dark.'

'There's a moon,' persisted Karen gently. 'It's full tonight. We must try, surely, just in case.'

'Of course . . . ' and another heavy silence fell as Karl gave the matter some thought. It was shattered by the shrill call of the telephone, making them both start at its strident intrusion. Karl picked up the receiver.

'Hotel Adler.'

'Herr Braun?'

'Speaking. Who's that?'

'Never mind. We have some property of yours.'

'Property?' Karl's voice cracked with emotion. He cleared his throat. 'What property?' Karen sat bolt upright in her chair, straining to try and catch what the caller was saying, but she could hear only the rumble of his voice, not his actual words, they were for Karl alone.

'Seventeen, dark-haired, wearing a gold watch on a chain round her neck.'

'Yes?' Karl's voice was scarcely above a whisper.

'We don't want her. We've got the wrong girl. We'll swap her for the right one.'

'What!' cried Karl. 'What do you mean?'

The voice continued as if Karl had not spoken. 'Don't contact the police or speak to anyone about this if you want your darling daughter back. She's no good to us, it's up to you whether you get her back alive. We'll call again.'

There was a click as the line went dead even as Karl began to speak again. 'No — wait . . . ' but it was too late. With great precision he replaced the receiver.

'They've got Marta — and they want to swap her for Charlotte.'

'Swap her!' exclaimed Karen incredulously. 'How can we? They must know you can't.'

'Of course we can't, but how else are we going to get Marta back?'

'The police, Karl, you must call the police.'

'I can't, they said if I called in the police I'd never see Marta alive.'

'But a swap . . . ' Karen shook her head in disbelief. 'How do they propose to set about it? The swap, I mean.'

Karl shrugged. 'He said he'd call me back, we can only wait, they could have her anywhere.'

'Herr Braun, you are wanted in the dining-room please.' Fritz's anxious voice broke in as he hovered by the door. 'Table six — there is some trouble with the wine.' Karl downed the rest of his brandy and rose reluctantly to his feet.

'I'm coming, Fritz.' He turned to Karen, his face set in the grim lines she had seen so often; now she realised they were part of his protection, his outer shell which hid all his inner feelings and emotions, not part of Karl himself.

'Are you changing for this evening's entertainment?'

'I usually do, but . . . ' Karen was about to say she would not be doing so now, but Karl said, 'Then please do. I want everything to look as normal as possible. We'll say Marta has gone to a party if anyone asks. I'll have to tell Frau Leiter and she'll say the same.' He went to the dining-room and Karen was glad he had something to do, no matter how trivial, like coping with Mrs Garfield's ill-educated palate, to take his mind off Marta in the hands of kidnappers.

Karen was just coming downstairs sometime later dressed in her ridiculous Bo-Peep costume when the front door burst open and a man strode in followed by a pale, slight woman. The man was tall and dark-haired; he had immensely bushy eyebrows that seemed to meet in a straight line above his nose. His eyes were deepset and wide apart giving him a slightly startled expression which was suddenly increased when he saw Karen on the stairs.

'Good Lord! Who on earth are you?'

Karen was taken aback for a moment at this greeting, until she remembered her absurd outfit.

'Karen Miller, Lambs International.'

'Do you all have to wear that peculiar rig?'

'David!' rebuked the woman with him. 'Really!' She turned to Karen. 'Good-evening. I wonder if you can help us. We're looking for Miss Emma Armstrong and her niece Charlotte.'

'Sir David and Lady Armstrong?'

Before they could answer Karen knew she was right for when she stepped forward into the light Lady Armstrong was clearly an older version of Charlotte. She had the same long fair hair, though hers was swept up into a chignon, leaving her face framed by a few carefully escaping tendrils. Her eyes were the same deep blue and her mouth was as wide and curving as her daughter's. 'They could be sisters rather than mother and daughter,' thought Karen and hoped she would look as good when she had a daughter Charlotte's age.

'Yes, that's right. Are they in the hotel?'

'Thank goodness you're here,' said Karen, feeling as if a tremendous weight had been lifted from her shoulders. Now there was no way that Karl could swap Charlotte for Marta. Had she really thought he might? It was a thought which had nagged at the back of her mind ever since she had heard the proposal and she had seen the desperation in his eyes. It was one which she had loyally and resolutely thrust from her. Karl would never consider such a thing unless driven to it by unknown depths of despair. Now with the arrival of Sir David and Lady Armstrong, it would be quite out of the question and Karen felt tremendous relief that Karl would not be put to the test.

'Yes, they're upstairs, I think — I'll call Herr Braun, the manager.'

'Don't bother, we'll see him later.' Sir David moved towards the stairs.

'I'm sorry, Sir David, but you must

see Herr Braun, it is most important.' She saw Fritz going into the bar and asked him to find Karl.

'Find him straight away, Fritz, and tell him Sir David and Lady Armstrong are here.'

'What's all this?' demanded Sir David. 'Now look here, young lady . . . ' His face took on a forbidding stare and he took a step forward as he spoke, but Karen stood her ground until Karl arrived. He led Sir David and his wife into the office, asking Karen to find Miss Emma and Charlotte.

On her way back downstairs Karen was waylaid by two of her guests who were looking for the kitchens in the hope of borrowing two aprons for their costumes. By the time she had been down with them and managed to secure what they were looking for and then joined the group assembled in Karl's office, he had already explained the developments. Charlotte was sitting in one of the armchairs looking very subdued and a little apprehensive, though she seemed in no way frightened by what was going on, rather it appealed to her sense of drama with her at the centre of the stage. Frau Leiter was there too. Everyone looked serious. 'What I would like to know,' Karl was saying in his careful English, 'is why these people should want to take away your daughter.'

'It is difficult to explain,' said Sir David, pacing up and down like a caged animal — never taking more or less than six paces in either direction; he reminded Karen of a polar bear she had once seen at Whipsnade zoo, padding a prescribed route over and over again. The effect was almost hypnotic.

'We know of your troubles in England, Miss Armstrong has explained.'

'Well that helps,' said Sir David, pausing for a moment in his pacing. 'I am known for my determination to withstand blackmail, from whatever direction it comes. Do you understand me?'

'If I do not, Karen will translate,' Karl replied.

'Ah, good,' said Sir David and from then on addressed himself to Karen. 'I have said I will not back down in the present dispute — I have offered all I can and most of the men agree, but there is a militant minority, a mere handful who are determined to make me give way and with as much publicity as possible. It's perfectly simple really, they take Charlotte and in return for her safety I back down publicly with no other explanation other than that I was wrong.' The sound of music wafted up from the keller-bar where the fancy-dress party was to be held. It was starting and at the sound of the disco Charlotte stirred in her chair. Her mother looked across at her and said, 'Go and get into your fancy dress, Charlotte, and go to your party.'

'But don't leave this hotel for any reason whatsoever,' warned her father. 'And you are to say absolutely nothing to anybody about what you have heard here. Understand?' Charlotte promised and hurriedly made good her escape from the gloomy office to the gaiety of the keller-bar.

Karen had quickly translated what Sir David had said for the benefit of Frau Leiter, then she turned back to Sir David.

'The unions are trying to kidnap Charlotte?' She was incredulous. 'That's really a bit far-fetched, Sir David. Trade unions don't go round kidnapping people.'

'Not the unions as such of course,' agreed Sir David, 'but there's a militant communist element in the one in dispute and they will stop at nothing to bring me down.'

'David is the kind of boss they hate the most,' put in Lady Armstrong, 'because he does pay attention to union complaints if he thinks they're justified, but he won't be blackmailed by strikes and the like.'

'But what I don't understand,' said Karen wearily, 'is how do you know about the kidnapping. Surely these people haven't warned you?' She was still unconvinced that such an idea could be possible.

'One of the more moderate men discovered the plan somehow and he was horrified that such a trick should be played. He had the courage to come to me and warn me. He also told me that the union had almost agreed to settle before but suddenly people began to change their minds. There was talk of intimidation.'

'There so often is,' remarked Karen drily.

'Agreed, but in this case I think it is probably true.'

'By the same militant minority?' asked Karen.

'By this same militant minority. And furthermore, now this has happened to me, I'm almost certain it must have happened to a colleague of mine. He was faced with extended industrial confrontation earlier this year and having braved it out for several weeks he suddenly climbed down and gave way to all the union demands.'

'Same union?' asked Karen sharply.

'Same union.'

'But he never said so?'

'How could he? It was almost certainly part of the deal to get his daughter or son back, and who'd believe him afterwards even if he did reveal it? But if I can expose such a plot and produce proof of what they tried to do I can give it such massive publicity nothing like it will ever be able to happen again, because, as we said, it's not the main body of the union involved. Ordinary, hard-working people would never condone such action. It's just a few fanatics, and,' Sir David's face was grim as he spoke, 'I'd give anything to bust them wide out into the open.'

Karl and Karen exchanged glances. It was difficult to believe such an incredible story.

'And now these people have Marta.' Karl's voice was flat, drained of emotion.

'I'm afraid it looks as if they do.

Obviously they discovered Charlotte's whereabouts, they are usually well informed. It was never a secret of course, but we always try to keep publicity to a minimum.'

'The problem is, how are we going to get her back?' said Lady Armstrong. Her voice was calm, a low even voice that soothed at it spoke.

'It sounds to me as if we can plan nothing until we hear from the kidnappers again,' said Sir David. 'They have asked for a swap, but until we hear how they plan to get away with it there is nothing to do but wait.'

'And when we do hear?' said Karl bitterly. 'What then?'

'That we can decide when we know more of what's going on. But depend upon it, Herr Braun, we'll do everything possible to get your daughter back and break these bastards. In the meantime,' Sir David looked round at them all, 'there are two things I suggest. One is that you all appear as normal as possible and the other is that our arrival is concealed as far as possible, so that we have the kidnappers believing that they only have you to deal with, Herr Braun.' Karl nodded at the wisdom of this and quickly pushed his mother-in-law and Karen into action. Frau Leiter was to produce food and drink for the Armstrongs, who would remain unseen in Karl's office, and Karen was to join the party in the keller-bar.

As the two women were leaving the room the telephone rang and they froze with dread anticipation as Karl answered it.

'Hotel Adler.'

'Herr Braun?'

'Speaking. Who's that?'

'There's a letter for you in the front hall. It tells you what to do. Be there. You won't get a second chance.' The phone went dead and Karl slowly replaced the receiver.

'There's a letter in the hall,' he said.

It was in a brown envelope and Karl's name and address were printed across it. It lay on the edge of Karen's kiosk and had arrived unnoticed by anyone. They had no idea who had delivered it nor how long it had been there. He ripped open the envelope and scanned the single sheet of paper it contained, then he handed it to Karen.

'What does it say?' asked Sir David, impatiently reaching for it.

'Do you read German?' asked Karen.

'No,' he admitted. 'Perhaps you'll translate.'

'It says, 'Start the chairlift at exactly 2 a.m. Place Charlotte on chair 1, Marta will be on chair 72 coming from middle station. Any funny business and we shoot both girls. Any sign of police and we do the same!'

'Is that all?'

'That's all.'

'So what do we do next?' Karl's former lethargy had slipped away and now he betrayed none of the despair Karen had read in his eyes earlier. His uncertainty was replaced by a burning desire for action and his question was more of demand than a query.

'We think,' said Sir David, apparently assuming command. 'You and Karen must go and take part in the festivities downstairs and perhaps Frau Leiter could find us some food as arranged. Then we meet here again in half an hour or so and see what ideas we can produce.' He pushed Karen towards the door and glanced at his watch. 'We have four and a half hours until the switch must be made. We must use a little of it to think.'

Karl nodded his agreement and Karen allowed herself to be eased out of the room. They made their way to the keller-bar where the New Year's Eve party was in full swing, leaving Frau Leiter to produce a tray of food for the Armstrongs from the deserted kitchen.

16

As they opened the door of the keller-bar they were enveloped in a blast of heat and loud music. Karen's Bo-Peep costume was greeted with hoots of laughter and, making a determined effort to appear normal, she joined in the party, accepting a drink from the henpecked Mr Garfield, now dressed as a portly Roman, apparently wearing little more than an enormous bath-towel and a wreath of ivy on his balding head. Mrs Garfield bore down on them from the other side of the room and Karen, feeling unable to face the miserable woman at that moment, smiled at her and escaped to speak to the leader of the little band. There was a roll on the drums and a hush fell over the room.

'We'll judge the costumes now,' announced Karen, 'before they fall into too much disrepair.'

Everyone laughed and three people not in costume were selected at random as judges. Sitting with Karen and Karl at a table, they awarded marks to each contestant as he or she paraded past them. Karen glanced across at Karl and admired the way he kept all trace of worry from his face; no one would suspect from his manner that his daughter had been kidnapped and was in possible danger of her life. Karen's heart went out to him as she mentally urged him to maintain such courage. She herself found her mind returning again and again to the thought of Marta alone and afraid, locked away somewhere, and she shuddered at the persistent thought. What Karl must have been going through did not bear consideration and she wished they were back up in the office with the Armstrongs doing something, anything, positive towards the girl's release.

The costumes in the parade were very good, many of them ingeniously contrived from a great many everyday objects to be found round the hotel. Several of the men had dared to appear in evening-dresses belonging to their wives and one of the girls had borrowed a pair of lederhosen. There was a burglar dressed in black sweater and trousers with a stocking pulled over his head and carrying a huge paper sack from the kitchen marked SWAG in bright red lipstick. Charlotte appeared in a red bikini, black tights and boots and she had made a little head-dress from gold cardboard covered with sequins. There was a sort of extended sigh from most of the men present, irrespective of age, as she cavorted across the room, doing a Wonder Woman twirl before the judges' table. Karen felt her own expression harden as she saw Charlotte positively basking in the adulation of at least half the room, but a quick glance at Karl showed her no sign of his feelings about Charlotte and so, repressing her own anger, Karen merely marked the girl's costume and looked up to see who was next.

At last the judging was over. Not surprisingly Charlotte had walked away with the women's prize, while the men's had been won by a man who had procured a walking-stick and bowler hat from somewhere and managed a very passable imitation of Charlie Chaplin's walk.

After the winners of the fancy dress had been announced, applauded and rewarded, there were calls for the promised party games and during the next half hour or so both Karl and Karen were in demand to organise them. Karl ran the beer-drinking competition, with teams of locals and tourists competing against each other. It was like a relay race and each member of each team had to drink a litre of beer, then, when the bottle was empty, place it on his head as a signal to his next team-mate to start drinking. There was a great deal of hilarity and spilt beer by the end of the competition which was ultimately won by a team of the younger ski-instructors, led by the inimitable Hans-Peter. Karen found herself laughing in spite of her agitation for Marta's safety and glanced guiltily at Karl, but he too was grinning as he watched the race, able to pretend the carefree enjoyment of everyone else. However, once the prizes for this had been awarded and Karen had organised one or two stupid team games, at last the pop-group began to play again and separately Karen and Karl were able to slip away from the festivities and rejoin the anxious group in the office.

Fortified by soup, bread and cheese, Sir David again took charge once they were all assembled.

'Right,' he said, accepting a brandy from Karl and lighting a cigar from his own gold case, 'anyone come up with anything?' There was an expectant silence while everyone waited for someone else to speak first. Nobody did.

'Well,' said Sir David. 'Let's begin

with negatives. I take it we're not sending Charlotte.' Everyone nodded in agreement.

'And I presume at the moment we leave the police out of it, as we don't want to risk further harm coming to the girl.'

'Surely we should tell them,' burst out Karen. 'I mean, we can't just leave poor Marta to the mercy of those men.'

Karl's eyes were dark with anger.

'We shall certainly not leave Marta, but I'm not sure the police are the answer. They must have Marta up the hill somewhere. After all they snatched her when she was out skiing and as they intend to be at the middle station they must be above it somewhere. There are hundreds of little cabins and huts up on the mountains that the farmers use in summer when the animals are in the high pastures. They could have her hidden anywhere there.'

'Suppose we appear to let the switch take place but when Marta is safely clear on her way down, and before

Charlotte has reached the top, we stop the lift,' suggested Karen.

'How would you get either girl down?' asked Karl. 'Remember, there are one hundred and forty-four chairs and so on the specified chairs they are always equidistant from the nearest lift station. If the lift goes forward with Marta to safety, Charlotte reaches the top and danger and, if you bring Charlotte back down, Marta is up to the top again. It's a clever switch.'

'Couldn't we start that way and leave the girls halfway while the police round up the kidnappers?' suggested Lady Armstrong.

'They've threatened to shoot if anything goes wrong. They have a clear view of one or other of the girls the whole time,' reminded Karl.

'But would they shoot?'

'I don't know, probably not but is it a risk you're prepared to take?' asked Karl grimly. Lady Armstrong lapsed into silence.

'I think,' said Sir David slowly, 'I

think we're going to have to accept that at least one of the kidnappers is a cold calculating professional, employed to do a job of work, but completely uninvolved emotionally with the militants' cause as such. Thus he is in many ways more dangerous.' Silence fell again as they took in what Sir David had said and recognised both the gravity and the truth of it.

'Couldn't the person going up get off the chair?' suggested Karen tentatively to Karl, speaking in German. 'You know, I mean that steep place in the woods where the ground rises so sharply under the chair that you're only about six feet above it.'

'Certainly possible,' agreed Karl, 'but you'd have to know exactly when to jump and it would be pretty dangerous even in daylight. Also of course, the other chair coming down would still be within easy reach of the middle station at that stage. I think that's probably out.'

Karen was relieved, because she had

the glimmer of an idea brewing in her mind and she was glad that jumping off a chairlift in the darkness did not have to form part of it.

'What are you all saying?' demanded poor Frau Leiter, frustrated at being unable to understand the part of the conversation conducted in English and longing to know what was being said. Karen translated briefly and Frau Leiter agreed with the no-police arguments.

'Is there any way of reaching the top of the chairlift without going up it?' asked Sir David after a moment.

'Not from this village,' said Karl. 'It is possible from the next one, Feldkirch.'

'Couldn't the police go in that way?' asked Sir David.

'They might,' said Karl, considering, 'but it would take time enough to get here from the valley. We can't risk going in with too few and I'm against involving the police anyway. We have to get Marta clear before we do anything . . . ' He paused and Sir David finished the sentence for him, 'And they won't put Marta on if Charlotte is not seen to mount the chair at the bottom.'

'Exactly.'

Another silence fell as they all considered the implication of this. Karen broke it at last by giving air to the idea she had been considering and said simply, 'I could go.'

'What?' They all stared at her.

'I could go. It'll be dark and if I dress in jeans and a sweater and anorak and wear Charlotte's fur hat pulled well down to hide my hair it might fool them long enough to put Marta on the chair.'

'But,' Karl began to protest, 'you're nothing like her. With good night-glasses they'll spot you at once. You're the wrong build and height and colour hair and everything. It's out of the question.' He spoke abruptly, dismissing Karen's offer with disconcerting finality. Karen felt the colour flood her face at his rebuke and lapsed into uncomfortable silence.

'I could go,' said Lady Armstrong

softly. 'I'm exactly the same as Charlotte especially with my hair down.'

Now it was Sir David's turn to protest, but his wife cut him short.

'Listen to me, David,' she almost snapped at him. 'It's our fault that Herr Braun's daughter is involved in this at all. The least we can do is risk a little to get her safely out of danger. I'm not suggesting Charlotte goes, of course I'm not, but I can go instead and intend to do so if we can work out how to capture these men waiting for me at the top of the lift.'

Karen could see Sir David was not used to his wife's making such important decisions, or telling him what to do, and he was taken aback at the determination with which she spoke. She glared round, defying any of them to snap her brittle courage, and each of them recognised the possibility of Lady Armstrong's being able to take her daughter's place, undetected by anyone with binoculars from the middle station. It was an outside chance but just feasible with careful planning and a lot of luck.

'They may be watching the bottom station,' said Sir David, 'it's too risky.'

'I expect they will be,' said Lady Armstrong calmly, now completely in control of the situation. 'But if Herr Braun pushes me about a bit and I am sufficiently reluctant so that he has to force me on to the chair we may convince them in the darkness that I'm Charlotte. After all they can't get too close or we'll see them!'

'That's true.' Her husband was beginning to accept the possibility of the idea, though the thought of his wife's risking her own neck for the sake of an unknown girl still made him hesitate.

'Can you think of another way?' Karl spoke sharply. 'Because if not we have much to arrange to carry this plan to a successful ending. For a start I have to persuade Heinrich to let me run the lift — he's not going to like that and may try to insist that the police are informed, to cover him in case things don't work out.'

Karen had been translating softly for Frau Leiter as the suggestion had been made, and now the older woman spoke.

'This lady has offered to help and we must accept gratefully, but only if we can arrange some way of catching the kidnappers at the top so that she comes to no harm. If the lift can be stopped safely halfway, with both at maximum distance from the lift station, then what? Remember they can start the lift again from the middle station. There is a switch at each end.' Karen translated again, this time for the benefit of the Armstrongs, and they all gave their consideration to what Frau Leiter had said.

'If not the police then who?' asked Karen. 'Who can get to the middle station undetected to catch the kidnappers or at least rescue Lady Armstrong when she reaches the top. No one answered her question and then she answered it herself.

'Of course,' she cried leaping to her feet, 'of course, Johann and the ski-instructors. Johann's very fond of Marta. He could go with a group and ski down from Feldkirch.' Karl nodded slowly as he considered the idea.

'It might work. There'd have to be enough of them.'

'And they'd have to be armed,' added Sir David.

'Armed!' cried Karen. 'Where would they get arms from? It's going to be awfully dangerous.'

'Of course there will be danger,' said Karl impatiently, 'we're dealing with dangerous men here and Marta's life is at stake, but we all have hunting guns here. Arms are no problem. We've all skied with a gun across our back before now.'

'But you can't go,' pointed out Lady Armstrong. 'You have to stay at the bottom with me. Anyway is it really possible to ski from this other place you said across to the lift here?'

Karl drew back the heavy curtains

and looked out of the window to the frozen night. The moon was full though often covered by scudding clouds, and the snow-covered mountains towered above the village, gleaming with strange reflected light.

'I should think so,' he said. 'It's not a difficult run really and it's a fairly clear night. Experienced skiers could certainly do it.'

'Shall I go and find Johann?' asked Karen. 'We need him here before we plan any further.'

'Yes, you're right,' agreed Karl. 'You go and fetch him, he's more likely to come if you explain it face to face, rather than using the phone.' As Karen went to the door Karl added, 'Don't forget someone may be watching the hotel. Make it casual. I should change first too,' he said with the ghost of a smile and Karen suddenly realised she was still in her Bo-Peep outfit.

17

As soon as she had dragged on her ski-suit and fur boots, Karen hurried back downstairs, then slowing her movements right down she sauntered out of the hotel's front door and crossed the square towards Johann's bar as she had done on so many other evenings. The square was still quite crowded with people out celebrating the New Year; there was a great deal of echoing laughter and music exploded from the crowded cafes and bars as their doors were opened to cram in more folk out in search of a good time. It was impossible for Karen to tell if anyone was watching her, but she took no chances and drifted along stopping to peer into cafes through their misted windows and glancing in at the shops, hoping to convince anyone who might be following her that she was in no particular hurry, and then strolled down the alley towards Johann's door.

The darkness in the little lane was pierced only by occasional shafts of light gleaming through unlatched shutters and tripping over a paving-stone Karen wondered why it seemed much darker than usual. Then she realised. There was no welcoming porch light burning outside Johann's door, his sign was lost in shadow and his windows though shuttered were unlit. The whole house was silently black. Though she knew there was no one there she tried the door and found it firmly barred against her. She felt round for a bell, but finding nothing she pounded on the heavy carved wooden door with her fists. The muffled thuds she managed to make produced no sign of life from within the house and so, puzzled as to why Johann's bar should be closed on New Year's Eve when other bars and cafes were crushed with noisily celebrating people, she crossed back to the hotel.

While she had been out Karl had managed to get hold of Heinrich the chairlift-operator. Karen found them both sitting in Karl's office discussing the situation. Heinrich's wizened face was the colour of dark leather, but from the creases deeply etched by time and experience there stared a pair of brilliant blue eyes, alert, direct and piercing. When he was concentrating he sucked on his bottom lip and expelled the air through his nostrils in exaggerated snorts. He was concentrating now, considering the problem laid before him by Karl. A glance from Karl warned Karen not to interrupt and she stood silently by the door until Heinrich spoke.

'You can run the lift,' he said at last, 'but I must be there.'

'But supposing they don't accept you too?' protested Karl. 'They may call the whole thing off if they think I'm not alone with the girl.' But Heinrich was adamant and Karl recognising this agreed that they both should go. Then he turned to Karen. 'Where's Johann?'

'Not there. His bar is closed and the whole house in darkness.'

'Not there?' repeated Karl, amazed. 'Are you sure? It's New Year's Eve, he ought to be doing a roaring trade.'

'Positive.'

'Well, we'll have to work without him,' said Karl. 'I'll ring the other instructors. You see if Hans-Peter is still in the keller-bar with the rest of his beer-drinking cronies.' Karen nodded and turned downstairs. Karl seemed calmly in control of the situation, she thought, and his steadiness helped her to keep cool, although she found she was attacked by little waves of panic that welled up within her. Suppose they were too late, or there was violence and Marta got hurt. Suppose the kidnappers actually got hold of Lady Armstrong; after all Marta would not be safely at the bottom of the chairlift until Lady Armstrong had arrived at the middle station and unless the rescue party timed their attack perfectly, when neither hostage was actually with the kidnappers, there was extreme danger for either or both Marta and Lady Armstrong. Sir David had said the men must have been being led by a professional, coolly and unemotionally detached, merely working for money, and such a one might well kill rather than allow himself to be caught. Fighting down these terrifying thoughts, Karen straightened her shoulders and continued on her way to look for Hans-Peter.

The warmth and the noise flooded round her as Karen forced her way into the packed keller-bar. The music blared unceasingly and voices were raised to a shout to enable even one's nearest neighbour to hear a word. There was a throng of people dancing on the small square of open floor and the tables and chairs round the room were packed with people and stacked with glasses. A heavy cloud of smoke hung over the room and discarded accessories to fancy-dress costumes were dangling from chairs or dumped in corners as their owners had dispensed with them after the judging earlier. Karen caught sight of Hans-Peter squeezed into a corner of the dance-floor hardly able to move with Charlotte, still skimpily clad as Wonder Woman, draped round his neck. Edging her way across the room she just reached him as the pop-group's drummer produced a loud roll on the drums.

'Ladies and Gentlemen,' he announced. '1980 is upon us, just ten seconds to go. 10 — 9 — 8 — 7 . . .' Everyone joined in the count-down, shouting the numbers in unison and ending at zero with a loud cheer. Someone started singing Auld Lang Syne and it was immediately taken up by all who knew it, then there was a great deal of kissing and laughter as everyone wished everyone else a Happy New Year. Karen found herself embraced from all sides by her guests and also by men from the village and other tourists whom she had never seen before. Hans-Peter was jostled away from her and Charlotte was lost in a sea of admirers, all eager to take advantage of their chance to kiss the beautiful English girl, Wonder Woman.

It was some time before Karen, flushed and slightly exasperated by the persistence of so many well-wishers, managed to clutch Hans-Peter's arm. He turned and seeing who it was grabbed her in a bear-hug.

'You're needed upstairs,' she cried as soon as she got her breath back.

'What?' He strained to hear her above the noise of the music which had begun again.

'Upstairs,' mouthed Karen urgently. 'Bring Charlotte.'

Sensing her urgency, Hans-Peter had let her go while he forced his way across the room to prise Charlotte from the arms of her admirers. How he managed to drag Charlotte away Karen did not know, but her dependence on his capability in that direction was not misplaced and they soon joined her at the top of the keller steps, Charlotte protesting strongly as usual at Hans-Peter's high-handedness.

'What's the problem?' asked Hans-Peter, still holding Charlotte firmly by the wrist as he spoke.

'Herr Braun will tell you,' said Karen. 'Come over to the office, it's about Marta.' Hans-Peter and Charlotte followed Karen across the hall, but before they reached the door it opened and Lady Armstrong came out to meet them.

'I need you upstairs, Charlotte,' she said in a tone that brooked no argument and taking her daughter's arm led her to the staircase, leaving Hans-Peter and Karen to join the others in the office.

'What's going on?' asked the young man, a little bewildered at the grave-faced group who were waiting for him, Heinrich, Sir David, Karl and Frau Leiter, all serious and silent.

'I'll explain in a minute or so,' said Karl, 'when the others get here. Are any of your friends still downstairs, your beer-drinking gang, I mean?' Hans-Peter shook his head.

'They've gone on to another party. I only stayed because Charlotte said she couldn't go.'

'Well I'm sorry to drag you away from the fun.'

Hans-Peter shrugged. 'I don't mind. It was getting pretty hot down there.' He perched on the arm of one of the chairs and looked enquiringly at Sir David. Karen introduced them briefly and then spoke softly to Karl.

'How many others did you get?'

'I've reached seven, that's eight with Hans-Peter. They're coming here at once.' Karen showed surprise and though she said nothing knowing Karl was stretched almost to breaking-point he answered her unspoken question abruptly.

'We have to have a definite plan that everyone knows. It's no good trying to relay instructions by phone. We must all know exactly what we are doing. I've warned them we may be being watched, they'll be careful.' He was standing close to her, speaking to her alone, his voice no more than a murmur. 'We have to trust them, we have no choice. Still no sign of Johann?' She shook her head and he put his hand on her arm. Looking up at him Karen could see the tiredness and anxiety in his eyes and a wave of warmth and love surged through her making her flush rosily and drop her eyes away. She longed to put her arms round this dark sombre man, rest her head against the comforting strength of his shoulder and coax a smile back to warm the bleakness of his face, and she was afraid that her longing must have been clearly reflected in her own eyes. But the moment had gone almost before it had come and he moved to the door to greet two of the instructors who had just arrived coming in through the keller-bar's outside entrance and up the indoor staircase into the hotel.

Softly the door opened several times more to admit the rest of the instructors Karl had called on and then once again to allow Lady Armstrong to slip through. For one moment Karen thought it was Charlotte who had come into the room, so like her daughter had Lady Armstrong made herself appear. She wore tight blue jeans tucked into long black boots, topped by a royal-blue polo-necked sweater. Her hair was caught into a pony-tail and knotted about carelessly with a matching blue scarf. Sir David at once went forward to meet his wife and pushed her gently into the chair he had occupied, then he turned to Karl.

'All yours, Herr Braun. Obviously it would be better for you to explain to your friends in German, so please carry on. Karen can translate when you come to the part that involves us.'

Karl nodded and turned to the expectant group crowded into the little office.

'I've already told you briefly what has happened on the phone,' he said. 'Marta has been kidnapped in mistake for this man's daughter. We have to try and get her back while appearing to arrange a swap, the right girl in return for Marta.' Quickly he outlined the plan to ski down from Feldkirch to the middle station of the chairlift above St Wilhelm, making sure they were not seen until Marta was safely on the way down and Lady Armstrong, standing as decoy for her own daughter, was safely on her way up. Then they had to try to overpower the kidnappers before Lady Armstrong arrived at the top of the lift. 'How are we going to get there without being seen?' asked Herbert Lang, one of the older instructors.

'You'll have to wait in the shadow of the trees just above,' said Karl. 'They're sure to search the immediate area before bringing her down to the lift, but once they have they should, with luck, be concentrating on attack from below rather than above. Once you're sure that Marta is safely on her way down on the chair you can ski down to the lift station and try to catch them.' He paused and looked round at them. 'Personally I don't give a damn if you catch them or not, all I want is Marta safe without anyone else taken hostage. We want no heroics, if you merely frighten them away so that both women are free that's all I care about.' There was a short silence while everyone considered what Karl had said and then Karen spoke, clearly and quietly.

'I'd like to go with the ski party,' she said and when her suggestion was greeted with cries of surprise and rejection she merely waited for them to die down and went on calmly, saying, 'If something goes wrong up there and anyone is hurt, I could be useful. If Marta is not safely on the chair and becomes involved in the attack or has been hurt in any way already, she'll need a woman there. I want to go too.' Hans-Peter grinned encouragingly and said, 'She skis well enough.' Karen could see that although Hans-Peter was well aware of the gravity of the situation he was excited by it, as if it were an adventure especially provided for his enjoyment; his eyes gleamed with excitement and his still boyish face was aglow with enthusiasm. She felt impatient with his attitude and hoped he would not get carried away and do anything stupid. Karl answered Karen as if Hans-Peter had not spoken.

'I don't think you should go, Karen. There will be little you can do that the others can't and it is stupid to expose yourself needlessly to danger.' Before Karen could reply Sir David said, 'If she wants to go I think she should. If the child is hurt and frightened she may need her.'

'No, Karen,' said Karl firmly. 'I cannot allow you.'

'You cannot stop me. Lady Armstrong is taking a similar risk. The important thing is to get Marta back safely and if I can help by going with the rescue party from Feldkirch I'll go.'

Her eyes held his as if they were alone in the room and though his look bored right through her she managed not to drop her gaze. Hans-Peter had been translating quietly for Frau Leiter and it was she who intervened in the duel between them. Speaking softly she said, 'Karl, my dear, I think, if she is willing, Karen should go. Marta may well be in a state of shock. She knows and trusts Karen.' She paused and added, 'I only wish I could go too. If I got my hands on those . . . ' Her voice trailed away, tired and dispirited.

'I want to go,' said Karen again.

Karl shrugged his shoulders, dismissing the affair as if it was suddenly of no consequence, and said, 'Then go. Now we must plan.'

Their plans were laid and in true commando style at Hans-Peter's suggestion their watches were synchronised. Timing was of vital importance for if they appeared before Marta was down on the chairlift she would be in great danger and if they left it too late Lady Armstrong would give the kidnappers another hostage. The ski-instructors slipped away to collect what they needed from their homes and were travelling in three cars to Feldkirch. Hans-Peter said he was going home to change and would come back for Karen in ten minutes and meet her by the ski-room door, away, they hoped, from any watching eyes.

Karen went upstairs to collect her ski-boots, gloves and hat and when she came down again she found Karl in the hall waiting for her. 'I'll come and unlock the ski-room for you,' he said and leading the way through the kitchens to the back door he took her out into the cold darkness and down to the ski-room.

'I won't put the light on,' he whispered, 'whereabouts are your skis?'

'On the left by the window,' she replied, her voice equally low.

They groped their way inside and Karl pulled the door to behind them before he flashed on a torch and its beam picked out the pattern of Karen's skis, clipped together with their sticks beside them. He moved them outside the door ready for Hans-Peter. Karen shivered in the freezing night air as they stood in silence waiting for the car. Karl felt the movement and very gently put his arms round her. For a moment Karen was too amazed to move and when she did his arms tightened, refusing to let her go, and his face was pressed against her hair. His shoulder was comfortingly close and Karen relaxed against him, resting her head against it and for a moment tasted the blissful safety and strength of his arms, just as she had so often imagined. She tried to look up and see his face but it was lost in the darkness. As she moved he released her and held her away from him a little.

'Karen — I . . . '

He was interrupted by the sound of a car and Hans-Peter drew up in the alley at the side of the hotel. Karl pressed his lips gently to her forehead as he had done before and said softly, 'Be careful up there, Karen. Don't take unnecessary risks.' He dropped his hands and turned to pick up her skis, handing them to Hans-Peter who clipped them on to the ski-rack on the back of his car.

'OK Karen?' Hans-Peter, still excited by the whole adventure spoke in a stage whisper that echoed through the darkness.

'Yes, I'm coming.' Her heart was beating so hard as she climbed into the car that she felt the two men must hear it. She wound down the window. Karl's hand rested for a minute on the open frame. On impulse she took it and pressed it to her cheek, saying softly as she did so, 'Don't worry, Karl, we'll get her back for you. You be careful too, so that you're waiting for her when she gets down.' Before Karl could reply Hans-Peter let in the clutch and the old car toiled away out of the alley and into the square, leaving Karl standing alone in the darkness, staring after it.

18

Hans-Peter followed the same route as they had taken in the bus, was it only the previous day? So much had happened that Karen could hardly believe that scarcely more than thirty-six hours had passed since they had set out at the beginning of the perfect day to ski across from Feldkirch. Now they were on the same road again, but this time it was night, with danger lurking in the darkness and the possibility of a girl's life at stake at the end of it. It made her shiver.

'Are you cold?' asked Hans-Peter. 'There's a rug in the back. I'm afraid the heater's not very efficient in this car, it only seems to blow cold.'

'No, I'm fine,' began Karen but gratefully accepted the rug Hans-Peter reached over from the back seat.

They drove in silence for some while,

Hans-Peter concentrating on the slippery twisting road, then he said, 'Lucky I was still at the hotel.'

Karen agreed and then asked, 'Where was Johann tonight? I went round there before I came down to find you. The bar was closed, the place dark and no sign of Johann.'

Hans-Peter shrugged. 'Never know with Johann, he's always got a list of willing females standing in line with him. Do you mind?'

The question was sudden, shot at her out of the darkness, and Karen was silent for a moment, apparently giving it some thought, then she answered coolly, 'No I don't mind. I was just surprised to find the bar closed on New Year's Eve, that's all.

Hans-Peter laughed. 'I expect he's up to mischief somewhere,' little knowing how truly he spoke, but in what different circumstances.

When they reached Feldkirch they found the lift-operator there waiting for them in answer to a phone call from

Heinrich in St Wilhelm. Karen had never been on a chairlift in the dark and as she swung out into the moonlit night the shadows jumped around her making it impossible to judge distances. It was bitterly cold and the wind which kept the clouds scurrying across the face of the moon cut through her ski-suit and the several jerseys she was wearing underneath. By the time she reached the top her hands, though protected by thick ski gloves, were numb and her face ached with cold.

They gathered together in a group waiting for everyone to come up the chair. The dark shape of the restaurant loomed above them and the terrace where they had eaten their lunch on that perfect day — was it only yesterday? — stood stark against the paler darkness of the sky. The moon sailed out from behind a cloud and suddenly everything appeared in sharp relief, black and silver. Herbert took charge. Though he was a very experienced man, Karen could not help wishing Johann were there. She thought about Hans-Peter's answers on the journey from St Wilhelm but did not quite accept them; she felt something was wrong. Now as they prepared to ski across the mountain with only the moon to light their way, Herbert spoke.

'This light is deceptive,' he began, 'and the last thing any of us can afford is a bad fall and a broken bone. There's no hurry if we keep moving steadily. We must keep in a line, and you, Fräulein, follow me.'

'He's determined I shan't trail and hold them up,' thought Karen, 'but so am I,' and she slipped into position behind him.

They sped off across the mountain following the route the ski-classes had used the previous day. Karen was very relieved that they did not have to shoot the gun-barrel as she and Karl and Marta had done yesterday. In broad daylight under a sunny sky it had been exhilarating to speed down the steep gully, but in the intermittent moonlight it would be a terrifying death-trap. Following Herbert was not difficult and her eyes had soon adjusted to the strange pale reflected light from the snow. Karen grew warmer as the blood coursed through her and, relaxing, felt something of the exhilaration she knew Hans-Peter and the others were feeling as they skimmed over the frozen mountain, negotiating the steep mogul-fields and narrow wooded trails with easy speed. No one spoke and the only sound was the hiss of their skis over the frozen crust of the snow. Herbert stopped several times to be sure no one had fallen behind, but the skiing was not hard and they were still close together. One of the stops was in the wood where Karen had felt that they were being watched the previous day. As they stood in the dark shadows now, the trees, cloaked in heavy snow and silence, seemed sinister and Karen knew she would have been afraid to stand there on her own. As it was she felt nervous as if the depths of those trees hid something malevolent. She wondered if Marta's kidnappers had indeed followed them yesterday, hoping for a chance to snatch Charlotte even then; perhaps it was he who shadowed them stealthily through the trees. She shivered. Herbert said, 'We must keep moving, are you cold, Fräulein?'

'No, Herbert, I'm fine,' replied Karen, determined to keep up at all costs as she knew Herbert, like Karl, had great misgivings about the wisdom of her going with them at all.

They skied on, following the trail through the woods which would at last open out on to the wide piste above the middle station of the St Wilhelm chairlift. Before they left the shelter of the trees, Herbert called a halt again.

'We must wait here,' he said in a low voice. 'Remember any sound will carry, so no noise of any kind, please.' He looked at his watch. 'We have only ten minutes to wait, then we should hear the chairlift start up.' It was the longest, coldest ten minutes in Karen's life. Well hidden in the trees they scanned the mountainside for signs of Marta and her kidnappers arriving at the middle station. Even when the moon sailed clear of the clouds it was difficult to distinguish more than the outline of the restaurant building and the chairlift station; the dark shapes melted together and presented only a vague silhouette. Hans-Peter came over to Karen and whispered, 'Can you see anything?'

'No,' she replied, 'but I don't know the terrain well enough to pick out the different landmarks.'

'Well, the chair is on the left, see, you can see the top of the last pylon to the left of the lift station. The restaurant is on the right and we shall approach with that between us and the actual lift station in the hope that they don't see us coming.' Karen knew the plan and recognised that the most difficult part of their approach would be to cross the wide stretch of snow between the trees and the back of the restaurant. For the few moments it took they would be exposed upon the broad white hillside, clearly visible to anyone who glanced that way.

'Listen!' hissed Herbert. They all strained their ears and heard the sound of the chairlift running. It came faintly in the clear night air, the whirr of the motor and the clunk-clunk as the chairs passed the nearest pylon. Karen peered at her watch. It was exactly 2 a.m. 'It's on!' she breathed and found her stomach seemed to have taken up gymnastics and her knees felt like jelly.

A chair would take about ten minutes to come up from the bottom station, but they could not be more exact than that as Lady Armstrong and Marta were to be placed on particular chairs and nobody knew where these chairs had been left when the lift closed on the previous evening. The minimum time, if chair number one happened to be nearing the bottom, would be ten minutes, but if it was just on its way up it might be double that time before Marta was safely away. Karen watched the hands of her watch creep round four minutes and then Herbert gave the signal to ski. Each man knew what he had to do, but all Herbert hissed at Karen was, 'Keep back and stay out of the way. If the child is there still, and it's possible, get her clear.' With these contradictory instructions he led the ski-bound rescue squad out into the clear pale light of the moon across the wide open snowfields towards the shelter of the restaurant's shadow. Karen kept pace with Hans-Peter as they all went at breakneck speed, clear black figures across the white expanse of snow, eagerly seeking the sheltering darkness awaiting them on the other side. Would any of the kidnappers look up from the lift station and see them coming? Karen found herself praying, 'Oh God, don't let them look, let them concentrate on the chair and the paths from the valley.'

Once hidden from the lift station, Herbert brought the little group to a halt again. Karen could feel the tense excitement barely contained as several of them removed their skis and unslung the hunting-guns from their shoulders. Karen and some of the others kept their skis on in case the kidnappers tried to whisk either Marta or Lady Armstrong away again. The sound of the chair was still a steady hum in the darkness and as there had been no cries of alarm or warning from below them Karen could only assume either that they had not been seen or that there was no one there.

Herbert climbed on to the terrace outside the restaurant from where with a pair of binoculars he could see the bottom station. The lights were on and he could see Karl standing watching the chairs through binoculars from the bottom. Herbert slipped back down to them. 'It's on. Karl's at the bottom looking up through his field glasses and that was the sign he said he'd give once Lady Armstrong was on her way up, so we hope we can assume Marta is on her way down.'

Those who had taken off their skis were led by the giant of a man, Klaus Werner, who had lifted Mr Short on the chair in Johann's bar. Moving surprisingly stealthily for so big a man, he edged his group forward and crept round the restaurant, crawling across the snow until they were on the rise above the lift station. From there they had a clear view of the flat area in front of the lift station. Klaus sent Hans-Peter back to tell Herbert and the waiting group that there were four men to contend with and no sign of Marta.

'One has a rifle trained on the descending chairs,' whispered Hans-Peter, 'presumably he's covering Marta. Two more are watching the woodland trails, one on each side of the station and the other is on the dismounting platform waiting for Lady Armstrong, or Charlotte rather, and he's got a gun too.'

Herbert nodded and sent Hans-Peter back to Klaus's group, telling them to cover the four men with their shotguns and wait for his signal. Hans-Peter slipped silently to the others, a ghostly black figure against the snow. Herbert allowed a further moment for his message to get through and then called out, 'Don't move any of you, we have you all covered and you're outnumbered two to one.' His voice echoed strangely out of the night. The four men all spun round towards the sound of it, but he was well concealed in the shifting darkness above them. 'Drop your guns and put your hands up,' ordered Herbert. For a moment or two no one moved and Klaus fired a warning shot into the air. At once the rifle and gun were thrown down and all four men raised their hands above their heads.

'OK, Herbert,' called Klaus and at that the rest of the rescuers sped down the slope on their skis to relieve the amazed men of their arms and to herd them into a close group until they could be tied and brought safely down the mountain.

As the moonlight struck their faces for the first time Karen gave a gasp as she recognised one of the captured men as Johann. All the instructors recognised him in the same moment and there were cries of astonishment and dismay. Johann stood like the others with his hands in the air looking round defiantly at his erstwhile companions from the ski-school. Karen couldn't believe her eyes. She continued to stare at Johann. What on earth was he doing there apparently completely involved in this terrible kidnapping? It made no sense at all and Karen was too amazed to credit it. She peered at the rest of the little group. In it she recognised the young man who had tried to pick up Charlotte at the Feldkirch restaurant. So that was indeed the first attempt to waylay her. 'What a lucky thing Hans-Peter is the jealous type, or we'd have lost her then!' thought Karen. Seeing the man standing gloomily beside Johann, both of them with their hands in the air, it came to her in a flash where she had seen him before. 'Of course,' she spoke aloud, yet under her breath, 'he was one of the men in Johann's bar, the ones he told me were from another tour operator. They must have been plotting this then. But where is the other one?' He was not in the forlorn little group surrounded by the army of ski-instructors. He was nowhere to be seen and Karen made the mistake of dismissing him from her mind as she puzzled as to why Johann should be involved in it all.

19

The chairlift continued to run and Karen moved to the edge of the dismounting platform to help Lady Armstrong off the chair when she arrived. Standing with her back to the darkness of the lift station she peered down the hill trying to see if anyone was coming up. Far below lights gleamed in the night showing where the bottom station lay and Karen realised that with good binoculars it would be possible to see someone mount the lift and perhaps even distinguish who he was. She glanced at her watch. Only eight minutes had elapsed since Herbert had given the signal to cross the open snowfield above the restaurant, eight minutes in which things had gone so easily that it seemed almost an anticlimax after all the tension which had built up before. It appeared that

Marta was safely on her way down to her father and that Lady Armstrong would be in safe hands when she arrived at the top. They all stood in silence, shotguns trained on the huddled group waiting with their hands up for Karl's call on the chairlift telephone telling them all was well below and Marta was safe and unhurt. But it was not the telephone which shattered the silence and jerked the strange tableau to life, it was a cry from Johann.

'Karen! Look out!'

Karen spun round at his shout and found herself staring down the ugly black barrel of a revolver. She recoiled and then stood as if transfixed. The man who held the gun was still in the shadows but his harsh voice was clear enough.

'Keep still all of you or I shoot the girl.'

Nobody moved.

'Now all of you throw down your guns.'

There was a clatter of metal on ice as

the weapons fell to the ground. The gun never wavered from Karen's chest and nobody dared do anything but obey the man's orders.

'You,' he called to Hans-Peter who was nearest him, 'fetch my skis and sticks from in the station.' Hans-Peter did as he was told, bringing the skis out to the man.

'Come slowly and put them on the ground by my feet and remember, one false move and the girl dies.'

Hans-Peter came slowly and laid the skis ready for the man to step into.

'Hold them steady!' he barked and Hans-Peter knelt in the snow holding them steady as the man stepped into the bindings, his eyes never leaving the stunned group of rescuers and his gun never wavering from its target, Karen.

'Now fetch me the rescue rope.'

Hans-Peter unhooked the long rescue rope which hung coiled on the lift station wall to be used in case of an emergency on the mountain.

'Make a noose.'

Still not daring to do otherwise, for Karen's sake, Hans-Peter obeyed and handed the man the rope with a noose at its end. He slipped the coils across his shoulder and then flicked the noose over Karen's head, letting it rest round her neck.

'Now, young lady,' he said, 'if you do anything stupid, I pull. You understand?' And he jerked the rope a little tighter round Karen's neck to show what he meant. Karen nodded dumbly.

He shouted at Hans-Peter, 'Get back to the others.' Then he spoke to his own men who were almost as amazed as their erstwhile captors at what had transpired.

'Right, move you lot. We're done here, it's every man for himself.'

The group broke free and each made good his escape as fast as possible; all except Johann. He dived, not for the safety of the woods like the others, but into the lift station itself and threw the switch to stop the chairlift. As the man saw the movement and realised its implication he spun round and fired at Johann, who fell to the floor with a scream and lay there moaning, and had his gun aimed back at Karen well before she had time to think of trying to escape. 'Don't move, any of you!' he barked at the astounded group. 'I'm taking this girl as my protection. If I get away unharmed, maybe I'll leave her unharmed — unless of course she does anything stupid, like trying to outski me, then phht!' and he indicated the noose round her neck. 'Remember I'm not afraid to shoot. Move!' and, jerking the rope so it tightened even more about Karen's neck, he started gliding off down the hill towards the woodland trail and the valley below and unable to do anything else Karen skied six feet in front of him all the way.

She could feel the rope firmly round her throat and it hurt her to breathe though in fact it was not yet tight enough actually to impede her breathing. She was terrified, but managed to concentrate on trying to ski at precisely the right speed. She dared not go too fast in case the man did not keep pace and the rope tightened further as he lagged behind, but he was urging her forward and she could hear the sinister hiss of his skis right behind her own. It was extremely difficult to see the way in the thickness of the wood. The trees were heavily laden with snow and with the moon once more veiled in cloud, very little light penetrated their depths. Once or twice they moved little faster than at walking pace, straining their eyes to distinguish the turn of the trail. They broke out from under the trees and were able to make faster progress across a patch of open hillside before plunging once more into the trees on the other side and following the trail that zigzagged below the chairlift. They were approaching the cut-off track which would ultimately lead them to the far side of the village. Karen wondered whether the man knew of that route which led away from danger, or if with her as hostage he would risk skiing the more direct route to the village, past the bottom station. If he was the professional Sir David had suggested he might be, he would certainly have studied the area and have an escape route mapped out.

They passed under the chair for the last time and as they approached the cut-off he said, 'Keep right here,' and Karen's heart sank as she knew they were headed for the far side of the village. He jerked the noose to emphasise his point, creeping up almost level with her as he urged her faster and sought to make her do what he said. Suddenly something wrapped itself round their knees and in a confusion of sticks and skis they were both tumbled into the soft snow. Karen lay half-stunned where she was for a moment face down in a snowdrift. Her head had hit something hard and was spinning in an alarming fashion. There was something heavy lying across her back and she was aware of the cold snow forcing its way down her neck and into her eyes, nose and mouth. She tried to turn her head but could not lift it clear because of the weight across her shoulders. Her thoughts came slowly and with great deliberation she told herself, 'I must move, or I shall suffocate in the snow.' But she seemed powerless to act.

All at once the weight was lifted from her and she was able to drag her face clear of the all-invading snow. Then as if in a dream she heard Karl's voice, far away and echoing.

'Karen! Are you all right? Karen!' She couldn't believe it was he, he was at the bottom station waiting for Marta, it must be all part of the same awful nightmare. How could Karl be there? She felt most confused but looking up she found his grim face peering down at her, his eyes fierce with anxiety.

'Are you all right?' With his knife he cut away the noose still trailing from her neck and she winced as the steel blade flashed so close to her throat.

She stared up at him and said at last, 'It was Johann.' Abruptly Karl left her as he heard movement from her captor. He too was lying in the snow, one of his legs twisted at a most peculiar angle. He moaned, but Karl gave him no time to recover. He gave him a sharp blow to his chin and then looped the noose-rope securely round the man's shoulders, binding his arms close to his body so that he was trussed like a turkey. Karen had closed her eyes and drifted off into semi-consciousness again, but she was aware of someone moving near her. She forced her eyes open and saw Karl stripping off his ski-jacket. He wrapped it round her and made a pillow for her head with his ski-gloves.

'Don't worry — help is coming. I'm here.'

The words echoed strangely in Karen's head, muddling themselves together. 'I'm coming, help is here. I'm help, I'm here,' and then a strange gloom surrounded her and with a last memory of Karl chafing her hands in his she slipped thankfully into the waiting darkness.

20

When Karen awoke she found she had been miraculously transported to her own warm bedroom in the Hotel Adler. The cold which she had felt seeping into her body out on the hard hillside had been replaced by a comfortable warmth and softness. The light from the window seemed overbright and she closed her eyes hurriedly again as it pierced her brain and split her head with pain.

'She's awake.' Somewhere in the distance she heard Marta's eager voice and was aware of a face close to hers.

'Marta,' she thought, 'Marta's safe. Thank God for that.'

In a rush all the events of the night before crowded into her mind and she realised that Marta was indeed safe and even now leaning over her bed. Karen forced her eyes open again and, by turning her head away from the window, found the light bearable at least.

'You are awake, Karen, aren't you?' The girl spoke urgently. 'You are all right?'

'Yes.' Karen found her voice came huskily. 'Yes, Marta, I'm awake and all right.'

Frau Leiter unceremoniously shooed Marta away and gave Karen something warm to drink. Karen swallowed a few mouthfuls gratefully and then drifted off to sleep again, only aware of the nagging pain in her head and the need to escape from it.

Frau Leiter had put a sedative in the drink and when Karen awoke again it was to find the afternoon sun streaming in through her window and Marta seated at her bedside reading a book. For a moment Karen lay quite still and allowed the memories of the previous night to flood back through her, and it all had a nightmare quality, a mixture of fear and unreality. Her headache had subsided from a sharp pain to a dull throb and she put her hand up to her head to find out exactly where she was hurt and discovered a very tender spot on the side of her forehead. Her movement caught Marta's attention and the girl's face split into a delighted grin as she realised Karen was awake.

'Are you feeling better?' she asked solicitously. 'You look awful still. I'll get Oma.'

She slipped from the room and by the time she returned with Frau Leiter Karen had heaved herself up on one elbow in an effort to sit up.

'Lie down again at once, you silly girl,' scolded Frau Leiter. 'The doctor said complete rest — you have slight concussion.'

'I'm all right,' protested Karen, though she did feel very weak. 'I'd rather sit up if you could help me with my pillows.' Still tutting, Frau Leiter plumped up the pillows and Karen sank back against them gratefully, but now feeling more part of her surroundings.

'Now, stay in bed,' ordered Frau Leiter, 'don't try to get up. Are you hungry? The doctor said you could have something light if you were. Will you try something?'

More to please the old lady than because she felt hungry, Karen agreed to try and Frau Leiter bustled off to heat some soup. Marta, warned by her grandmother not to tire her, remained with Karen, sprawled in the chair by her bed.

'Tell me what happened to you,' said Karen when they were alone. 'How did you manage to get yourself kidnapped?'

Marta pulled a face and said, 'They thought I was that silly bitch Charlotte!'

'Marta! Don't call her that.'

'Well she is.'

Karen let it pass and said, 'So, what happened? Were you in her suit?'

Marta had the grace to look sheepish. 'Well, yes,' she admitted, 'I did borrow it for the afternoon. She wasn't using it and it is rather super.'

'And they thought you were Charlotte?'

'Yes, I was coming down the back route from the top of the second chairlift and on the narrow part I was overtaken by two skiers going very fast. Something was thrown over my head, a blanket, I think, and of course I fell. Luckily I'd heard them coming fast and had slowed to let them pass, so although I fell it was not at tremendous speed. Then someone put some awful-smelling rag to my face and I passed out.'

'Ether?' suggested Karen.

'Probably,' said Marta. 'I don't know, it smelt like hospitals.' She wrinkled her nose at the recollection. 'The next thing I knew I was in Johann's hut. I think they took me there on the blood-wagon.'

'Johann's hut!' exclaimed Karen. 'Of course, he was there.'

'Well he wasn't to begin with,' said Marta. 'It wasn't until he turned up that they knew I wasn't Charlotte. I hadn't told them who I was because I assumed they knew. I didn't know they wanted her not me.'

'What did Johann say?' asked Karen.

'He brought me some soup and told me to pretend I didn't know him and then he told them who I was. Another man had arrived with him and he was furious at the mistake. He was obviously the boss, they were all scared stiff of him. Anyway, they left me locked in the bedroom part of the cabin and had a confab next door. It was jolly cold — they had the fire.' Marta seemed remarkably unscathed by her ordeal, telling her tale with enthusiasm.

'They'd given me this soup and a couple of rolls and then later, when it was dark, they skied me down to the middle station, I was on the blood-wagon again, firmly strapped on so that I couldn't try to escape. I wasn't going to anyway, because Johann had told me I was going to be exchanged for Charlotte.'

'Did you know how?' asked Karen.

'No, we got to the middle station and I had to wait with Johann while the other men searched the place, then we went down and waited. We saw the lights go on at the bottom station and the boss man with the binoculars said Daddy was there with Charlotte, and to watch for any tricks. The lift started and they told me I was going down, but unless I sat absolutely still till I got to the bottom they'd shoot me. I believed them too! One man had a gun, but it wasn't him who threatened me, it was the boss man. I didn't like him, he really scared me. Then he said, 'There's the signal. Look for the chair.' And suddenly Johann pushed me forward and said, 'The next chair. Tell your father I did what I could. Keep your head down!' I sat on that chair not daring to move and went down the hill. I heard a bang but I didn't dare to turn round. We were nearly at the bottom station and then the chair stopped, then there was another bang, the phone rang in the bottom station and then the lift started again and I went on down to the bottom where Heinrich was waiting.'

'Heinrich?' asked Karen, astonished. 'But where on earth was your father?'

'On his way up to you,' replied Marta, simply.

Karen looked at her face, alight with excitement now that it was all over, and could only wonder at her resilience.

'Have you seen the police yet?' she asked.

'Oh yes, Daddy had them here this morning. They wanted to see you too, but he wouldn't let them.'

'Johann!' said Karen suddenly. 'Something happened to Johann.'

'He was shot,' said Marta, matter-of-factly. 'He's all right, he's in hospital.'

'What about Lady Armstrong?' asked Karen faintly.

'Oh, they've gone, thank goodness. Packed up and left today. Good riddance, I say.'

'Yes,' thought Karen, 'I bet you do.'

The bedroom door opened again to admit Frau Leiter, carrying a bowl of soup, and Karl with an enormous bruise on his cheek.

'Now, Marta,' said Frau Leiter, 'you've tired Karen enough. Off you go, there's a good girl, you can see her again tomorrow. Complete rest, the doctor said.' Her final comment was directed at Karl as she hustled Marta out of the room.

Karl had taken the soup from his mother-in-law and now seated himself in the chair that Marta had vacated.

'You'd better have this,' he said, 'or there'll be hell to pay. Can you manage or do you want feeding?'

'I can manage, thank you,' began Karen indignantly, but the bowl shook in her hands and Karl took it back and held it for her while she spooned a few mouthfuls from it. Then she lay back and shook her head.

'That's enough, thank you.' He put the bowl down and said, 'Are you feeling better?' She didn't answer his question, but raised her hand to the livid bruise on his cheek, a deep purple smear already yellowing at its extremities. She touched it gently.

'How did you come to get that?'

He grimaced. 'I made rather sharp contact with that man's skis when I was stopping him,' and without further preamble Karl took her hand and turning it palm upward kissed it gently. 'I was afraid I was going to lose you too.'

Karen looked up into his face and saw his eyes intent on hers and in those eyes she saw such love and tenderness that she had to look away again, overawed that any man should look at her that way.

Without releasing her hand, Karl moved from the chair to the edge of her bed and taking her other hand said, 'Karen, my little, brave Karen. Look at me. Last night before you left me you gave me such hope that you might feel as I do. Don't look away.'

She raised her eyes once more and, seeing his love reflected there, he pulled her into his arms and began to kiss her in the way she had never dared to dream of. His arms were strong, holding her to him as if he would never let her go, and safely within them all Karen could do was to cling to him and return his kisses in a way which left him in no doubt of her feelings. At last he raised his head but kept her cradled against him, his face pressed to her hair, and said softly, 'I love you, Karen. If I had lost you last night . . . ' he left the sentence unfinished. Karen pulled herself free of him and then, resting her hands on his shoulders, said, 'I love you, Karl, more than anyone I've ever known.' He smiled his special smile and said, 'It was worth any risk I took just to hear you say that.'

'Tell me,' demanded Karen, leaning back against the pillow, her aches and pains long forgotten, 'tell me how you came to be there so miraculously. I couldn't believe it was you.'

'Mother-in-law told me not to tire you,' Karl said quite seriously and then they both exploded into laughter as they imagined what the old lady would have thought about the scene two minutes earlier.

'Please tell me.'

'Well.' Karl kept her hands prisoners in his as he described what had happened when the chairlift had stopped.

'As soon as it slowed down I knew something was wrong. Then the connecting phone rang and Hans-Peter burbled something about Johann being shot and you being a hostage.'

'What on earth was Johann doing there?' interrupted Karen. 'Why was he involved at all?'

'Money,' replied Karl. 'It appears that when his father died last year he left Johann with a mountain of debts and the bar mortgaged to the hilt. These jokers came along and offered him a substantial sum to lend them his hut for a few days, to keep them fed and watered and act as a guide, no questions asked.'

'Didn't he know what was going on?' asked Karen, amazed.

'He knew it was something shady, obviously, assumed they were hiding people on the run or something. It wasn't until he saw Marta, and more to the point realised she would see him, that he was in real trouble.'

'You mean she would be in a position to identify him?'

'Yes, and that was a position of extreme danger as far as she was concerned, because although he wished her no harm, he's really very fond of her, he was not in charge of the operation, he was just the guide and her knowledge could endanger them all.'

'What did he do?'

'He kept out of Marta's sight until he had to take her in some food. Then as he was alone with her for a moment he told her not to recognise him if she saw him or he had to speak with her again.'

'So the others didn't know she knew him?'

'No. He merely said he knew she was my daughter and that they'd got the wrong girl.'

'Who suggested the switch?' asked Karen.

'I don't know, but I imagine it was

Johann, trying to ensure that Marta was returned to safety. Only he would see how it could be accomplished the way it was, none of the other men were from round here.'

'What about the boss man?'

'Working on a contract, but even he doesn't know who his real employers were. He worked through a go-between. He was the only real professional among them, the others were just petty crooks who could ski, and Johann was the dupe.'

'What'll happen to Johann now?'

Karl shrugged. 'Well, he's in hospital at the moment and after that it'll be police custody and trial. He'll have the fact that he saved Marta in his favour, he may not get too heavy a sentence.' Karl's eyes were bleak as he spoke.

'He did try to stop the chairlift before Charlotte appeared,' pointed out Karen tentatively.

'And got shot for his pains.'

'Yes, but it did warn you something was wrong and stop the boss man from being provided with another hostage. Lady Armstrong can't have been far from the top of the lift by that time.'

'No, that's true,' conceded Karl. 'Marta was almost down when it stopped.'

'You didn't wait to see her,' accused Karen gently.

'What, stand about down there when I could see Marta was all right, while you, according to Hans-Peter, who telephoned in panic the minute he dared, were being carried off as a hostage with a noose round your neck? Should I have waited for Marta?' He smiled quizzically, his grip on her hands tightening.

'No. At least I'm very glad you didn't!' admitted Karen fervently. 'Tell me what you did do. I still don't understand how you got there in time.'

'Well, when I heard what had happened from Hans-Peter I told him I was coming up the chair and would get off at that place in the woods where the slope is steep and the chairs are only a few feet off the ground. I told him to follow you at a safe distance but in no way to hustle or crowd you. I didn't want you in further danger, but I thought I might need help quickly.'

'It was slow going in the dark anyway,' said Karen. 'There was virtually no light on the woodland trail and neither of us knew the trail very well.'

'A good thing too,' returned Karl, 'I was counting on that. If you had I wouldn't have been there in time.'

'He said he'd let me go at the bottom,' said Karen. 'I wasn't in much danger. You took an awful risk jumping off the chair.'

'The risk of you getting to the bottom with that man was much more. Don't forget you could identify him. He had a gun and had already shown he wasn't afraid to use it. He would probably have used it to silence you when he had reached the safety of his car and you weren't any more use to him.' Karen shuddered involuntarily at the thought. Karl saw, and smiled reassuringly at her. 'But don't think about that now. You're safe.'

'What happened when you'd got off the chair?' asked Karen. 'I've only the vaguest of recollections of the whole thing.'

'Well, as I got onto the chair at the bottom I grabbed the first-aid pack and the emergency rescue rope from the lift station. I wasn't wearing skis, of course, so it was quite an easy jump really. My main worry was not being in time; that you'd have passed already.'

'I dropped the first-aid kit and the rope and then jumped after them. I seemed to make a terrible noise as I landed, I was terrified that I'd warned him.'

'We didn't hear anything,' said Karen. 'At least I didn't, I was concentrating on following the path and not letting that rope pull tighter round my neck!'

'I listened for a moment, but I didn't dare waste time, so then I got to work. In the darkest place I could see, just before the trails divide. I used the rope as a trip-wire. I tied it to the trunk of a tree and then hid the other side of the track. As you skied over the rope I pulled it tight with all my strength.'

'And tipped me unceremoniously into a snowdrift, knocking me out on a tree-stump or something.'

'Exactly. But my biggest fear was that in the fall the noose would pull tight round your neck, but I decided if I tripped you both there was less danger of that than if I went for him alone and you skied on dragging the noose tight by your own speed. I was only just in time. I could hear you coming before I was hidden myself.'

'What happened to him?' asked Karen with interest.

'He broke his leg,' replied Karl briefly and then added with a twinkle in his eye, 'and he had several bruises to his face.'

'You beat him up?' Karen was incredulous.

'Don't put it that crudely, darling,' answered Karl, 'but I was afraid he might escape before Hans-Peter, Herbert and the reinforcements arrived.'

'With a broken leg?' remarked Karen wryly.

'I didn't know it was broken then,' said Karl innocently. 'And I wasn't feeling too friendly towards the man who had tried to rob me of the two people I love most in the world.'

'What happened to him?' asked Karen.

'Oh, he's safely with the police. It turns out he was quite a popular gentleman, wanted in several different places. With luck he won't be about again for a long time.' Karl was silent for a moment as if considering what to say and when he did speak again his voice took on a soft but serious note.

'Karen, I loved Anna, my wife, and when she was killed I felt cheated and lost. I want you to understand why I must mention her now.'

'You must have loved her very much.'

'I did. And now I love you and I want to ask you to marry me, but I never want you to feel I'm comparing you with Anna. She was Anna and you're you, and you're quite different people. You're not some sort of substitute.' He paused and then went on. 'And I want you to be sure you're not thinking of Roger any more.' Karen was startled.

'Who told you about him?'

'Marta told me one day when we were talking about her heartbreak over that young puppy, Hans-Peter.'

'Well, she had no right,' said Karen hotly.

'I'm glad she did,' said Karl, smiling, 'it gave me hope. You had seemed so distant, so unapproachable — I could then believe you were anti-men in general, which cut Johann out as well as me.'

'I wasn't unapproachable — I just felt it was better to keep on business terms with you. You were the man I had to work with, and,' she added with a gleam in her eyes, 'impress.'

'Impress! Why impress?'

'Because you thought I couldn't do

my job. Because you wanted a man!' Karen felt a flicker of anger at the injustice of it even now, her face coloured. Karl laughed at that.

'How do you know?'

'I heard you tell Frau Leiter the evening I arrived.'

'Well, you know what they say about eavesdroppers. Anyway, by then it was too late.'

'If you really want to know,' said Karen in a small voice, 'I haven't thought about Roger very much since I arrived here. He's not important any more.'

'But what about us?' asked Karl.

Karen hesitated a little and then said, 'We haven't known each other very long. Only a month.'

'How long does it take?' asked Karl gently, looking steadfastly into her eyes. 'I knew that very first evening that you had shattered my carefully built defences. The lonely ache inside had gone and you were there in its place. Could you put up with me,

Karen? Will you marry me?'

Karen felt herself trembling with a sudden rush of happiness and, unable to speak, she nodded her reply, reaching for Karl as she did so.

'God, Karen,' he said thickly as he crushed her in his arms once more. 'Marry me quickly, for I can't live long under the same roof without you.'

'What about Marta?' she asked, when at last she was able to ask anything.

'She'll be pleased, I'm sure,' said Karl cheerfully. 'She's very fond of you.'

'As a friend, yes, but as a stepmother?'

'Why not, you'll make a beautiful stepmother.'

'But suppose there are children?' persisted Karen.

'I hope there will be,' replied Karl. 'Lots of them, and we shall enjoy every moment of getting them, my darling, I promise you.'

Karen tried once more to make him consider other factors.

'What about Lambs?'

Karl gave something remarkably like a snort and said, 'Who the hell are Lambs?' and he began kissing her again, holding her tightly as if he feared she might disappear. So Karen gave up trying to discuss such matters and concentrated on letting her beloved Karl know how entirely she reciprocated his feelings. There might be problems to be faced and overcome in the future, but for the moment she was in the arms of the man she loved and the man who loved her enough to have risked his own life to save hers. With love like that to build on their future seemed assured.

THE END

Other titles in the
Linford Romance Library:

IN THE HEART OF LOVE

Judy Chard

Alison Ross's humdrum life is violently changed when kidnappers take her daughter, Susi, mistaking her for the granddaughter of business tycoon David Beresford, in whose offices Alison is employed. The kidnappers realise their mistake and Susi's life is in danger. Now Alison's peaceful existence in the Devon countryside becomes embroiled not only in horror, but also unexpected romance. But this is threatened by spiteful gossip concerning her innocent relationships with the two men who wish to marry her . . .

OUT OF THE SHADOWS

Catriona McCuaig

Newly single and enjoying her job as an office temp, Rowena Dexter sees new hope for the future when she starts dating barrister Tom Forrest. But memories of a terrifying childhood incident resurface when she receives threatening e-mails. She was in the house when her aunt was murdered, and the case has never been solved. Rowena's former husband, Bruce, agrees to help her unmask the stalker, but can they solve the mystery before the murderer strikes again?

CHATEAU OF THE WINDMILL

Sheila Benton

Hannah's employer, a public relations agency, has despatched her to France to handle the promotion of a Chateau which is to be converted to an hotel. However Gerrard, the son of the owner, resents the conversion, and some of the residents of the Chateau are not what they seem to be. Now she begins to find herself entangled both in a mystery that surrounds a valuable tapestry, and also a Frenchman's romantic intentions . . .

BRAVE HEART

Diney Delancey

Glad to be leaving London and many unhappy memories, Janine Sherwood moves to Friars Bridge to take up her post as headmistress of the village school. Living in the house owned by school governor Sir Gavin Hampton, Janine and her daughter Tamsyn are comfortably established there. But shadows from the past reach out to haunt her — threatening to shatter the happiness she and Tamsyn have found. Danger surrounds Janine as she fights to save all she holds most dear.

AMELIA'S KNIGHT

Valerie Holmes

Amelia and her sister Ruth have mixed feelings when their impetuous mother decides they should stay with her sister, Sarah, in the harbour town of Whitby, for Amelia cannot envisage them finding suitable husbands there. However, once she has set eyes upon the gallant, but mysterious, Samuel Knight, Amelia's opinion changes . . . But her father, Archibald, an intelligence officer in pursuit of villains and a chest of stolen government gold, views Samuel in a rather different light . . .